NOTIC

To those whose dogs are missing, I have sad news.

They have joined a legion of like-minded souls. Do not try to find them because, if you succeed, you will encounter great danger, for they are,

DOGPYRE!

DEDICATION

I dedicate this book to the innocence,
bravery, empathy, and love that
canines possess in such great abundance.

ACKNOWLEDGEMENT

I wish to thank John Stafford whose patience and high standards
helped make this book what it is.
And, also a big thank you to Jo Ann Rooney and her dog, Nigel,
whose neighborhood antics provided welcome inspiration in the
creation of The Dogpyre Syndrome.

This book, and the series to which it belongs, would only be half
complete if it not for the beautiful design and layout, along with the
illustrations, conceived and drawn by my wife,
Carol Tippit Woolworth.

TipWorth Press • ISBN: 978-0-9852645-2-9

THE DOGPYRE SYNDROME

By

Sandy Woolworth

Illustrated by

Carol Tippit Woolworth

dog – pyre
noun (also **dog – pire**) (pl. **pyres** or **pires**) a canine that
has been transformed into a vampire like being

DERIVATIVES
dog – pyr – ism noun
ORIGIN Mid 18th cent.: from French (as a noun): from Proto-
Romanian, perhaps from Turkish *uber*

T|W|P
TIPWORTH PRESS

Prologue

On a bright, sunny day in July of 2010, in building X21 at the DuPont Experimental Station in Wilmington Delaware, Paulette Espin, a bio-molecular chemist working on food contaminants, combined two molecules, one from corn and one from the red kidney bean, altering the phytohemagglutinin present in the bean. The experiment was a success from the chemist's point of view; her objective was to modify the coagulation of red blood cells in mammals that is caused by phytohemagglutinins. The resulting material, labeled Phyto

710 was locked away in a secure refrigeration unit until other parts of the contaminant experiment were ready.

In January of 2011, Billy Winstock, an animal rights activist, maneuvered his Sea Eagle 124smb inflatable boat up the Brandywine River to the site of the DuPont Experimental Station. Under the cloak of a cold, moonless night, he broke into building X21 thinking it was building P21, the primates building. Once inside he realized his mistake.

With the building's alarm blaring, there was no time to go back and locate building P21 so he thought about what he could do to take advantage of his error. Billy's flickering flashlight was his only light source, and his map of building P21 was useless, so he decided to enter the first door in the hallway after the lobby. It was the refrigeration room lined wall-to-wall with Forma 8600 Series 40C refrigeration units designed to keep their contents at sub-zero temperatures indefinitely. He opened the first one he came to and grabbed a Thermo Biotransport test tube carrier that held, among other items, Phyto 710.

Billy ran out of the building as fast as he could. The inflatable boat that he had dragged onto the bank was just outside the hole in the chain link fence cut the night before. DuPont's security team was fast on his heels and Billy was scared. As he squeezed through the fence he caught his boot on one of the jagged, cut links, fell onto his head, blacked out and rolled down the bank into the rapidly moving Brandywine. The test tube rack, once tightly gripped by the fleeing Billy, broke open in the water spilling its quickly-defrosting contents as the glass tubes hit the rocky river bed. Phyto 710 bonded to the surface of the algae growing there and became part of the river's makeup. An unconscious Billy rode the rapids with his limp body and drowned.

In July of 2011, a full year after the creation of Phyto 710, a bat echo located water below, swooped down with its mouth open and drank from the Brandywine river.

Play Misty for Me

Things were different. I couldn't quite put my toe-nail on it, but they were. I barked at Reynaldo, it was 5:20 AM after all, and he popped up as usual, swiveled around swinging his feet out of bed to face me while saying cute things in high-pitched human speech that morphed into a song. I've always liked this greeting because it sets my mood for the day to come. It made me forget everything that was bothersome (bathroom, food, my territory, other dogs). With an awakening like that I had no choice but to ride that wave of cheerfulness.

Then a rustling sound presented itself from the far side of the bed. Another head popped up and I vaguely knew that head, but couldn't solidly place it in my thoughts. It was Francine and she now lived with Reynaldo and me. I knew it was Francine because of her aroma, a wonderful odor that I latched onto, filling my head with a feeling similar to thought. This odor meant something important to me, but what was it? I was concentrating because even though I knew the name, the odor, the look, I didn't know why Francine was important to me.

She looked at me with a delightfully pleasant face. Everything was slanting upward and her teeth were highly visible. A smile. I've always been a sucker for things like smiles and laughing and high pitched happy voices. I was getting good feelings from her, but I get good feelings from most people. Let's face it, when you're a dog in a wheelchair most people are nice to you. So "nice" wasn't what was intriguing here, what captured me was my memory ache. (A memory ache would be the exact same feeling a memory produces, but without the actual memory. It's something you get when you're not capable of memory, or at least long-term memory. I'd consider short term to be more my style. Moment to moment would be my motto, but important long ago events and beings did somehow linger.)

If, by some chance, you were able to read some of my DOGSPEAK* retrievals from a year ago, you'd remember a lot about Francine and me. You'd know the depth of our love and how wonderfully she took care of me. She even cooked for me. But now, because of certain life changing events that occurred last year, she looked at me like someone who wasn't quite sure what to make of dogs. With her stilted touch, a little hesitant, but sincere, I felt that, deep down, she liked canines. But I was confused. My feelings were enthusiastic toward her yet I could see no reason for this enthusiasm.

My mind had drifted enough. We finished the waking up ritual and now it was time to be carried downstairs to the kitchen. Reynaldo gently picked me up, cradling me like a baby. We passed by the mirror near the bedroom door and I caught a speedy glimpse of us as a unit. I saw how close his head was to mine, ready for a kiss right between the ears. I also saw the blur of our movement and the sleeve of Francine's bathrobe following close behind.

Then down the top floor stairs, through the hallway to the kitchen stairs and finally, liberated to my spot on the floor by my bowls. Reynaldo made coffee for himself and

* An explantation of DOGSPEAK appears on page 71.

tea for Francine. Once these morning delights were on the boil, he picked me up and carefully lowered my thirty pounds into the wheelchair. Next we went along the side of the house for a quick utility walk. Normal and routine. Nothing out of the ordinary.

With our first few steps outside it seemed to be just another average day in Wilmington Delaware. But as we progressed the air became extraordinarily thick with a misty fog, an entirely new experience. I must say I did not like this fog at all, a particularly opaque fog, with an odd odor and I've liked almost all odors in my time. I've been particularly fond of "off" odors, and as humans might put it, the "off-er" the better. But this one was an affront to my odor bank and it made me quite weak. My front legs wouldn't work. Reynaldo, ever conscious of my condition, rushed us back inside, picking me up, wheelchair and all. He practically threw me through the kitchen door. Reynaldo's never been rough before so something must have been terribly wrong.

Francine was at the door. Her features were downward, not smiling at all, and the kitchen smelled of the misty fog.

I could see through the full-length window in the kitchen door that the back yard was now completely filled with mist and as I watched, the yard disappeared.

I was frightened. I think Reynaldo and Francine were frightened too. This was not good; though maybe it's the way it's supposed to be, I don't know, but I really didn't like this. I was so weak and nauseous that I wasn't even thinking about my breakfast and neither were they.

Francine freed me from my wheels and I was lying down on my side. Both Reynaldo and Francine were on the floor, too. We never do this at breakfast time! The mist oozed in under the door. Strange. Such a sneaky mist, yet so dreamy.

My head moved an inch, all that I could muster, and I saw Francine's eyes, which were gazing into mine, turn white and then close. I was also losing my vision as I experienced a series of little blackouts and micro dreams of horror. My last dream was a vision of what can only be described as the ultimate of evils. A garbage truck starting and stopping, air-braking with abandon, right next to me. This, without rival, was my greatest fear, brought to me by this last, quick blackout vision. And then nothing. I was out. We were all out, and the kitchen was no more.

I Bark Therefore I am

...the next day

It was so bright in the bedroom, too bright to sleep because someone had turned on a light, so I raised my head to see if anything was happening, such as: Were Reynaldo and Francine still sleeping? But what's this? They're not there! I was alone. I didn't get a chance to use my subtle but instructive wake-up bark. I needed to "go out" but that was impossible on my own, so I just put my head back down and waited.

My mind drifted away from the immediate disappointment of not seeing anyone in the bed, drifted to my stomach, which was making noises, then drifted to my discomfort "down there," leading me back to where this all

began: needing to "go out." Who knew how long that took, but no matter now because I heard someone approaching the bedroom door. It was Francine, full of high-pitched tones and upward featured face, teeth showing and radiating positive energy directly at me.

She walked over with less of a limp than when she first arrived a few months ago, the lingering, traumatic effects of the air disaster we had all survived.

Air disaster? Well, I guess I can't let that go unexplained. We, the three of us, "the pack," were flying to England and our plane crashed into the Atlantic Ocean. They were in the proper part of the plane with the rest of the humans, and I was crated in the hold with a couple of other poor souls. We ended up in the water, me dog paddling in the ocean, the two other dogs inert, and many humans floundering about or just floating around whilst sleeping. (I say whilst because we were on our way to England.) Simply put, I floated to Brighton Beach (England) and was saved by the kindness of strangers. Francine was nowhere to be found, but Reynaldo and I eventually linked up and he brought me home.

She didn't surface until much later when Reynaldo and I went to Paris, and by chance met up with Francine, who was suffering from amnesia as a result of a bang on her forehead during the crash. After many weeks we convinced her to come home and get proper therapy. Reynaldo was very persuasive, but it was ultimately my

charm that clinched the deal. Anyway, between the two of us it worked, and now we're all together again.

Francine bent down to my bed and lifted me up so that my head rested on her shoulder, cradling my posterior in her left forearm with her hand supporting my left side. She patted and stroked me as her right arm braced my upper back below my neck. I mention these details because this is the first time she's carried me downstairs since she arrived. I loved it of course, and I was getting that old familiar feeling from her. There was her aroma comforting me, stirring some distant memory of maybe my birth mother, Hannah — well, no, not really. Hannah smelled like a dog, like me, but there was a new dimension to this that I couldn't figure out.

That's, of course, the whole problem, isn't it? I couldn't figure things out. I didn't dwell on this for I was extremely happy and felt very warm and safe from within. As we trekked out of the bedroom, I passed the mirror's reflection of us, with Francine's long black hair, some of it draped over my head with my right ear poking through, as my snout touched the glass leaving a long horizontal stripe of Winnie to delineate north from south.

Our trip down the back stairs, through the kitchen and onward to the dining room, was filled with petting and delightful high-pitched sounds. I not only heard them but I felt them as the vibrations came through Francine's chest and into mine as though we were one.

Dinner At Eight (AM)

Francine and our friend, Dr. Paulette Espin, appeared to be having a dinner party. At least they were sitting around the dining room table with an abundance of food that Reynaldo had just brought in. (I call any gathering in the dining room a dinner party no matter what time of day.) This one happened to be very early in the morning, a day after our little lie-me-down on the kitchen floor.

Francine had gently placed me under the table and I was all ears, (you know corgis, we are quite large in the ear department) listening for food mishaps. A typical example of this would be a glass of liquid catches a sleeve and, oh my, here's a puddle to lick up. Anything but wine or water I'd consider a licking event. Another example would be breadcrumbs, which, to my ears, sound like an avalanche of miracles. So you can see how I would have been riveted to my spot under the table. I wasn't there to eavesdrop, just to eat. But what was said went into my great big corgi ears and there's just nothing I hear that a DOGSPEAK retrieval won't reveal.

"We're analyzing the mist using fluorescence spectrophotometry in an air matrix, sampling the water, and in general spinning our wheels trying to figure this thing out. Lots of departments are working on it, but my group is the main one. It's really chaotic. I had to come over here partly to get my mind centered, and to make sure you're all right, Francine. Oh, and did I forget you, Winnie and Reynaldo?" Paulette said teasingly as she moved her chair closer to the table.

Francine smiled at Pauline, as she petted me with her foot, and replied, "Oh, well, my head's always in a state of something so I can't say that I feel out of the ordinary."

"Good then. Nothing different. I feel relieved. I'll confine my worrying to the lab, which is in turmoil. I can't think straight with all the hubbub going on, but we have discovered that Phyto 710 is clearly at the core of this. Francine, the salt please?" said Paulette somewhat tiredly. Reynaldo had scrambled some eggs and made lots of toast slathered with unsalted butter, not Paulette's favorite. She's a salted butter girl.

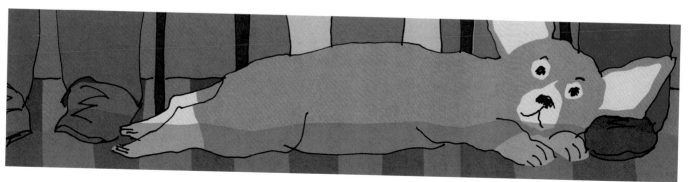

"Oh Paulette, it must be awful to think one of your experiments had something to do with this. Here's the salt. Oh no, Reynaldo, quick! Get some paper towels," said Francine after her arm had knocked over Paulette's glass.

What did I tell you, pass the salt, knock over a glass of what? Wine? No, not at this hour; orange juice. The natural thing for me to do is lick it up, and the natural thing for Reynaldo to do is clean it up before I can.

There we were, the two of us under the table, one to ingest, one to divest. The race had begun. Me lapping at a very fast pace. He gently backhanding my snout out of the way so he that he could sop up the Rorschach of nectar with his battery of paper towels. I nuzzled under his hand to get another lick in. It was a power struggle but he was winning. Then I started biting at the paper towels. They tasted of sweet oranges, or, well I don't know what an orange is, but they did taste sweet and considering how many times I've shredded paper towels without "orange" flavoring, this was a real delight. Add in the fact that Reynaldo was on the floor with me under the table and things just couldn't have been better. I thought we were playing, although Reynaldo did seem intent on getting me out of the way.

"It started with that break-in, don't you think? Is there any kind of proof that it was the Winstock guy who did it? Could it be some other thing that got in the river?" asked Reynaldo, who looked straight at me. I was looking at the paper towel in his hand, ready to pounce if he got distracted.

"No Reynaldo, it's phyto for sure. The river samples bear that out. There's no doubt at the lab. When the robbery happened we began sampling the river daily to record the changes taking place and the unanimous conclusion was that no harm was done and it was safe. Until yesterday, that is. Now we're thinking that it's something to do with the properties of water vapor that we weren't on the lookout for. We don't actually have a dense fog like that very often, do we?" she said as she mopped up the spilled juice in front of her. "The police are canvassing the neighborhoods near the river for other victims. So far no one seems to have had any side effects after their initial blackout. And everyone reports about the same time span of unconsciousness. If I weren't a chemist I'd find this very eerie," she said.

"We find it eerie. The mist was so thick, you literally couldn't see your hand in front of your face. And I'm a little concerned about Francine. We don't want anything to interfere with the progress she's making," said Reynaldo.

"I'm OK, Reynaldo. I told you this morning, everything's fine. I can remember everything just the way I did before the mist," said Francine.

This little exchange was just the distraction I needed to grab the paper towel out of his hand and drag myself away as fast as possible. Reynaldo, now flipped onto his side, was doing a long reach for my snout. I clenched tightly. I would not yield! The paper towel was shedding golden drops of sweet liquid mixed with paper towel flavor, a flavor you may not be acquainted with, but it's good. His hand was now all over my snout and three of his human fingers, so deft at paper towel removal, snatched it away. I had retained a tongue-sized portion in my tightly closed mouth and he couldn't get in there. My own private Idaho.

"Winnie," said Reynaldo in a low, controlled voice, not angry, not menacing, but meaningful. This is how you speak to a dog in my condition. This is the only upside of being paralyzed, the getting-away-with-it so to speak. No one utters an unkind word to me. Still, I'd rather be able to run, or at least walk.

"Paulette, I can't remember, did you say something about blood tests when you called earlier?" asked Reynaldo.

"Yes. We've set it up at the hospital so everyone in the neighborhood can walk over there to give a sample. Just walk in. We want to be very sure nothing is lingering in anyone's blood," said Paulette.

"I guess you didn't know what was going on where you and Parsi live," said Francine from the kitchen, as she looked out the window over the sink at what was now our sunny and mist-free backyard.

"No. Let's see, I was in my kitchen emptying the dishwasher and was about to feed the beast," Paulette's beast, Parsi, is a wolf. We've played occasionally and have known each other since puppyhood. There've been some fights over food, no blood though. Playful fights I guess. Who can remember?

They lived far away in the suburbs. Far away from the park and the river and far away from the reach of the mist.

"Nothing at all happened where we live. Actually, nothing ever happens in the suburbs. Not only am I bored out there, but Parsi seems to be getting a little antsy lately. I know the weather has been aggravating his arthritis. I've upped his dosage of aspirin, which may be upsetting him somehow. You know, either the aspirin or the arthritis is a problem. He's so sensitive. It could also simply be that he needs more space," said Paulette, as she salted another piece of toast to be eaten on the go.

"This has been so nice. The eggs were perfect, just what I needed. I guess I'll go back to the lab and see if there are any other disasters I can be a part of." And with that Paulette helped bring the dishes into the kitchen with Francine and Reynaldo before she left the house. I stayed right where I was because there was important crumb removal to attend to.

Howlin' Wolf

The crowded sidewalk in Wilmington was driving me crazy. People, milling about everywhere, kept rubbing against me as Paulette and I made our way back to the car. They patted my head and ran their hands along my back. Some actually pulled my tail. Did they think I liked this? I assumed my size was the big attraction-155 lbs. and over six feet long from snout's tip to tail's end. I was definitely a curiosity. This was both my misfortune and joy to be born into such a body, the body of one really big Alaskan wolf.

Paulette, my primary, weighed about 110 lbs and though she had my complete obedience, that fealty was something I'd given to her and could take away at any time. She wasn't alpha to me. I have always been my own alpha and the trade-off with her was my acquiescence for steady food and companionship. Notice I didn't say shelter. My skin and my thick fur are my shelter.

Life started with Paulette looking down at me as I emerged from my mother. I was born in captivity, and have benefited from it. Now as an adult wolf I had grown used to my daily routine, even though I constantly griped about it in the back of my mind. And there was lot to gripe about. For example, I knew I shouldn't accept food that I didn't stalk and kill. I knew I should roam my own hard-won territory, not some human's idea of my territory. I knew I should be leading about 4 or 5 other wolves and enjoying their subservience and submission, and I knew I should mate.

I had a strong need to dominate, so this domesticated life gnawed at me. Of course this wasn't articulated in my brain per se, but rather this was how DOGSPEAK 1.7 interpreted my feelings on the subject. And what I felt was a tension in my mouth. I wanted to lift my flaps and bare my teeth all the time, even to Paulette. I wanted to tear apart a

living animal and eat it. I wanted to select something really big, stalk it, organize my pack for an ambush and then sink my teeth into its neck, bringing the animal to the ground and tear away its flesh while growling furiously, not only for the food it provided, but for my own dignity. And when completely satisfied, I'd signal my pack to come ahead and

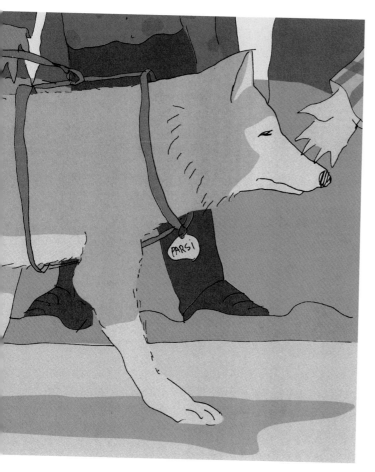

eat. And after gorging on this noble animal, I, in the most impassioned way possible, would howl. This is what I longed for all the time, an impassioned, meaningful howl. Not my usual howl at the moon, or my howl to broadcast my existence, but a howl that proclaimed my supremacy.

That was my ongoing theme – my essence – and this could never happen as long as I lived with Paulette. As a result, I was always looking for an opportunity to run away. The problem was Paulette. She may not have been the alpha, but she was a human, and humans did seem to have an edge in the smarts department.

Of course I wouldn't bite or threaten her in any way. I've been trained and one doesn't go against one's training. Plus there was the love factor; she's my mom. But if the door to our house happened to be open I'd be ready to move. If I did escape the house though, there would still be the gated, fenced-in yard. That gate was sacred, never left open. There was a buzzer on it just in case, but it had never buzzed. No one could approach the house without calling first. No accidents, no escape.

The only possible chance of escape would be during a car trip, a journey we'd take into town at least once a week. I enjoyed this because it broke the monotony of life in the suburbs. And even though the town's people touched and petted me, and it was annoying, I still got stimulated by being around so many living-breathing animals, human and otherwise. I even fantasized that I might run into a caribou or a massive elk because, in my Wolf's brain, anything was

15

possible. And on the way to town there have been deer both laying on the road or foraging in the fields beside the road.

Paulette could have done me a great service if she would've simply stopped the car, let me out, and let me be me. I could have easily caught one of those live deer. I'd kill it, eat it, lift what's left in my jaws to shake it and throw it. That would have meant so much to me. It would have brought a little bit of my Wolf-ness back. Then I'd come directly to the car without any coaxing at all. It needed only have been a once a year thing, on my birthday, for example. Why couldn't she have seen this.

On my last trip to Wilmington, driving by the field where I'd seen many a deer, the car started to get very unsteady. So much so that Paulette pulled over to the side of the road next to a ditch and stopped to see what was going on.

"Oh Parsi, I think we have a flat," she said. I was on full alert, but I didn't know what for. Just ready. I tensed up. My ears were at full height and my tail was straight out over the driver's seat. Something was about to happen and I could sense it was going to be good.

She got out of the car and came around to the tailgate. "Yup, it's flat!" she said. I positioned my body to face her. My back legs hunched down just a little and my head was stretched forward as far as it would go. Paulette now had her hand on the tailgate handle and unlatched it. The gate's hydraulic arms slowly lifted it open. Her stay command resonated in my head, but not in my heart. I looked into her eyes and then to the field beyond. I saw a deer. That's all it took. I leapt from the car, knocking Paulette into the ditch. I heard the usual stop and stay commands but was past responding to anything human. Immune to my training, I ran faster than I've run since I was a puppy. I ran and ran, the deer loomed closer. I could

smell it, and was completely consumed with its breath, its sweat, its fur, the whole living, breathing, vulnerable animal-ness of it all waiting for my carnage. Just a few more feet and I'd be on top of it. I got ready to leap and then I heard Paulette. "Parsi, stop!" She yelled, and this ingrained, pavlovian response mechanism kicked in just as

16

I was ready to sink my teeth into the neck of this very surprised deer.

I was so confused by all of my feelings — wolf-ness of bite, meek-ness of obeying — that I missed the deer's neck, knocking it over instead. I then tripped over it and hurt my neck. Pain had always enraged me and all I saw was red.

When her next 'stop' command arrived, it had zero effect. I got up and ran into the nearby woods. I knew she was chasing me, maybe the deer was too, but neither was my equal. Fast and alive! Free for the very first time in my life. What an unbelievably great feeling, to be wild, to be a wolf, to be me!

Winnie and the Bats

Tat-at-at-at-at-at. That's what I heard every night when we went for our 7 PM walk during the summer months. Over the neighborly conversations and noise of the passing cars, Tat-at-at-at-at-at floated high over-head and into the uppermost range of my hearing. Tat-at-at-at-at-at was strongest near the street lamp on the corner of Tatnall and Winchester streets where masses of flying insects swarmed around their sun god. I won't sit in judgement here; we K-9s can be eccentric in our behavior too.

As I gazed at them, along came a bat making its own Tat-at-at-at-at-at sound. It scooped-up a mouthful of insects and quickly glided away to make another pass. Not a bird, a bat. I knew the difference between bats and birds (I've eaten a few birds off the sidewalk). Birds have beaks, but bats look just like a corgi except they are smaller and have wings.

As Reynaldo and I continued our walk I noticed a bat on the street near the sewer grate. It was inert, a bit flattened and looked different from the bats overhead. Strangely, I had no desire to eat this animal. Usually I would have lustily gobbled it up, and, had it not been for the fact that it didn't smell right, I would have.

In most instances a slight whiff of decomposition would be all it would take for me to get excited about a new food opportunity, but this bat offered no wonderful whiff and what I sniffed was so disturbing that I ran from the area, pulling at

the leash attached to my wheelchair, yanking Reynaldo's arm in the process. I had to get away from that dreaded smell, one identical to the smell of our misty day a short time ago. The smell that brought our neighborhood to a standstill for several hours, leaving our minds blank, rendering people insensate. What a day! And so, now comes this inert bat, carrying that same wicked smell.

And another thing, this bat had fangs. Fangs the size of two-penny nails. Fangs that, considering its beautiful

symmetry and corgi-esque features, distorted an otherwise quite attractive face. But I've digressed. We were running because of me, not Reynaldo, who hadn't a clue when it came to odors. We were running toward home, toward the side of the house, toward the gate in the back yard and we were almost there when out of the sky, silently and with a malicious purpose, came one of those two-penny bats. It dive bombed onto my back and connected with such force that the wind was knocked out of me. It sank its fangs into my skin and then into the muscle next to my spine. I screamed and Reynaldo whacked the thing away with the back of his hand.

I've been through many attacks, many battles, paralysis, a plane crash, even survived the media, but I have never, ever, felt such an awful pain, such a sharp, every-nerve-in-your-body-on-fire pain, in my life. And then there was the matter of did I deserve this. I didn't provoke this in any way, either by a certain provocative look or by any action of any kind, and yet I got attacked?

And Reynaldo's hand swat wasn't the end of it. Easily ten more flew in to finish the job. Had Reynaldo not picked me up, wheels and all, I would have been Swiss cheese!

We made it to the kitchen pronto mismo and slammed the door just in time to foil the remaining luftwaffe. They crashed into the glass at full speed and with full bat fury. Some dropped to the ground and remained still. Others twitched and became inert, while three remained alive, able to generate enough electricity for me to notice their living, yet demented, presence.

Reynaldo attended to my one wound and then got on the phone to Lord David.

"David," he said in as calm of a voice as he could muster.

"Hello Reynaldo, are you all right? You sound a little stressed," Lord Northridge said. He always prided himself on picking up on other people's vibes, although Reynaldo's tone was quite a give-away.

"Winnie was just attacked by a very bizarre bat, or group of, I should say," Reynaldo said as he sat down at the island in the middle of the kitchen. "Could you come over?

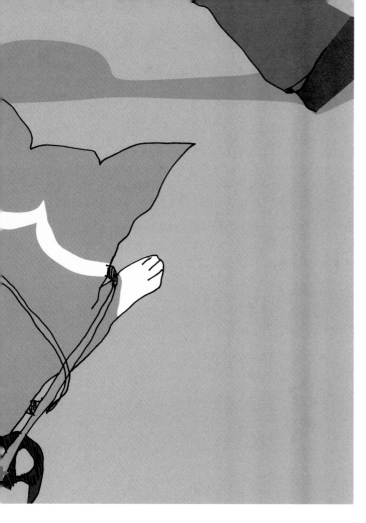

new wound was. And my focus was, well, not focusing. I was sensing things in an entirely different way. My vision was blurring slightly and my lower canines began to ache a bit. Oddly, I wasn't thinking about food, treats, people, attention, or any of my usual standbys. I was more caught up in the strange sensation of the increasingly muddled state of my brain.

Paulette and David gave me a very appropriate greeting consisting of one half of a milk bone from David, and some sort of little kibbly thing from Paulette. Surely she wouldn't give Parsi a treat so tasteless and insignificant. Surely she didn't think, "Oh, little Winnie, let me find some tiny, ridiculous thing to give to you, because you're so small." I have always resented this type of sizist thinking, especially when I imagined the enormous treats she must give to Parsi. I ate their treats anyway, but simply out of habit, not out of interest. Oddly enough, another wasn't wanted. My tastes were changing.

The three of them, Paulette, Lord David, and Reynaldo put on Platex Living Gloves and went outside to collect the dead and wounded, placing them in Tupperware containers Francine had given them.

The living bats were feisty but no match for living gloves. The dead possessed a poignancy unexpected by the three harvesters. There was a certain expression of sadness mixed with misery on each toothy little bat face.

Of course everyone was thinking "rabid bats". So next on the agenda was a trip to Dr. Cougar's to test the little devils for any sign of that dreaded disease. Little did they know how dreaded a disease could be.

There are three still alive and a few dead ones that I think you should see. I'm calling Paulette next. I think there could be some connection between the mist and these weird bats. Sort of a long shot, but why not check out anything that's a little weird, right?" he said as he walked over to the back door to inspect the dead and wounded on the mini battlefield outside.

Twenty minutes later Lord Northridge arrived followed by Paulette. Francine, already alerted to my adventure, was holding me on her lap.

I felt fine save for a funny, cold sensation where my

Into the Woods

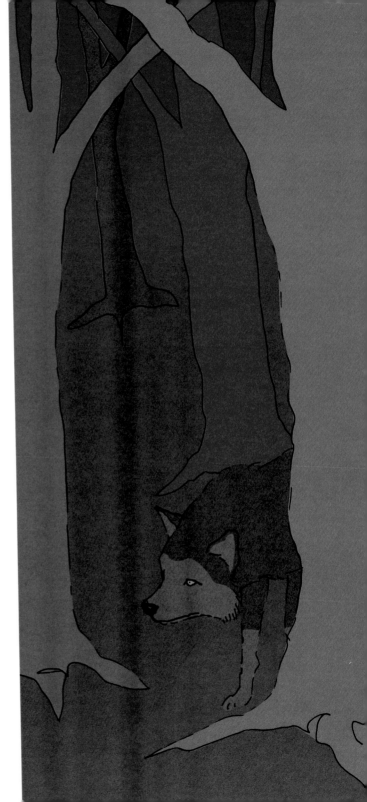

The chase was over. I couldn't see, hear, or, most importantly, smell Paulette or the deer. Was the deer ever chasing me? Just the fact that I didn't know if a deer would chase a wolf angered me. Having been domesticated from birth had left me with an awful lot to learn.

The woodsy environment was another thing that was totally alien: no real path laid out for me to follow; no obvious constructions for shelter; no food stations or bowls or even people to fill them. But what was I complaining about? This was what I'd always wanted. This had been my dream since birth. I needed to be patient. Getting used to so many new shapes, shadows, smells, sounds, and textures would take some time.

My new direction through the woods had taken me farther and farther away from Paulette and the field in which I last saw her. There was little doubt in my mind that food would come my way, that my body would provide all the shelter I'd need, and the lost companionship of Paulette would be replaced by many subservient wolves following my lead.

So far, though, I hadn't run across anything resembling a moose, an elk, a deer, let alone a wolf. There was only a squirrel here and there, scattering at the sound of my heavy footfall as I moved forward to dog knows where.

Because I was going against my obedience training when I ignored Paulette's stop command, I submitted to my panic mode. I realized that panic had its place in my survival arsenal, but it could also lead to great misfortune. I had to be extra cautious on this journey.

I. Kan't

As far as I knew Reynaldo had always picked me up like a little baby, cradled me in his arms, kissed the top of my head and taken me outdoors to my large, customized cardboard box, (similar to the one I was born in) which fitted perfectly in the back of the station wagon. This scenario was the same no matter where we were going if we were going somewhere in the car.

My enthusiasm for this stemmed from one thing and one thing only: the certainty of a treat. Just the thought of a carrot or some dry, baked, cube-like substance kept me in heaven for the entire ride. I wouldn't have specifically gone through all the possibilities of what it might be, how much of it would there be, what would it smell and taste like, how soon would I get it, would there be multiple treats, etc. I just dwelt fully on the thought of me getting a treat.

If someone took the time to analyze what actually happened during a treat event, they would discover that, one: I didn't taste said treat because after a cursory chomp I swallowed it as quickly as my tongue and esophagus would allow, and two: once the swallow had taken place, I'd forgotten all about that treat and was totally involved in the anticipation of the next one.

It could be deduced from this research that it didn't matter what you fed me. It was all in the getting. Just notice me. Notice me with food gifts. Be aware of my presence. Be thinking of me. ME!

The fact was, I was here purely for the pleasure of being me. Any displeasure that may have come my way would quickly be forgotten because it would only get in the way of my real purpose, my awareness of me. Humans might say, "It's my pleasure to help, serve, know, etc. you." I, dog Winnie, would say, "It's my pleasure to be served, noticed, fed, petted, walked, cared for, protected, hospitalized, fawned over, adored, and cleaned up after — by you."

Psychologically speaking, I have only one-third the psyche of a human. I have the id covered, but not the ego or the super ego.

We canines have solely desired whatever feels good at the time, all the time, no matter what the situation. We've lived for our senses, not for ideas. We'd take in huge amounts of data from our senses, and each sense, say, smell for example, would be complete in our thoughts in its own right. We wouldn't take in what we're smelling, seeing, feeling, etc., put it all together and then create a thought or get a new idea out of that information. Canines can't create the way humans do. Instead we'd use our multi-senses to locate items of interest such as a rival, a mate, or, most importantly, a morsel of food.

The eighteenth century Scottish philosopher David Hume said all of our experience of the world came from our senses. Of course, he was talking about people, but he came awfully close to how we canines think.

The German philosopher of the same era, Immanuel Kant, said humans perceived every thing through the envelope of time and space. (The philosophers Hume and Kant were introduced into my retrieval by DOGSPEAK v 1.7,

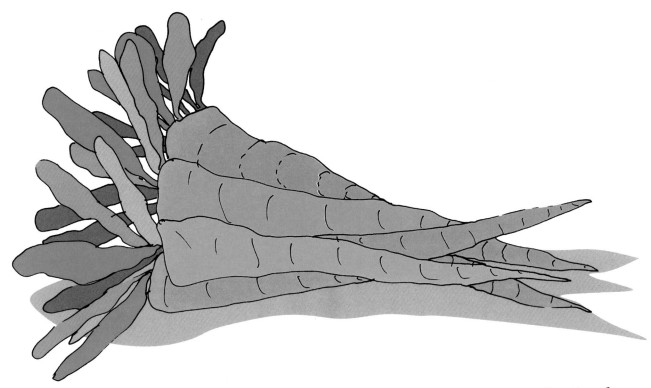

I know nothing of this.) Time and space were way beyond a canine's thought process. Kant was way off as far as we canines were concerned, but Hume was right on the money. We couldn't go beyond the present, and we could barely remember the past; though there might be a little twinge of memory or instinct thrown in just so we could function and survive.

Perhaps this is all very interesting to you who are learned...but I've only been to obedience school and my thoughts were centered on that treat, whatever form it might take. I heard treat noises emanating from the front seat and I really couldn't put this any more delicately — I was flat out drooling. Nothing to be embarrassed about because drooling was the direct manifestation of my philosophy.

This "canine philosophy" held true and was rock solid right up to the moment of that first bat bite. I had such a strong sense of self, a corgi's sense of self to boot, that it was difficult for the attack on my blood cells to alter or change me in any way. But the bat injected some very strong medicine and, slowly-but-surely, I responded in what was to become typical fashion in the days to come for all of us who were so afflicted. I was slowly changing into a Dogpyre. Yes, I still craved the treat that Reynaldo was about to give to me, but there was a craving for something else too. Something I would never have imagined. I was craving blood.

We're Not In Kansas Anymore

I, being a wolf, had no idea how long it had been since running away from Paulette and the deer and I, being in the present, marveled at the loud noises barking from within. And when not barking, my stomach growled with a ferocity I was not used to. No food had been provided, either as the daily gift from Paulette or by the field I was passing through.

Perhaps, because of the noise and constant movement of the vehicles on the nearby road, everything I could hunt and eat had been frightened away. Maybe there never were animals here in the first place, but something had to happen soon because my energy was abating. I was slowing down, and a wolf should never be slow.

Not remembering would be my normal state of being. I am now, not then, and most certainly not later. But I did recall some thoughts that were inexplicably connected to my life's milestones and high points. For example, it was easy for me to conjure up Paulette in my mind's eye, imagine running up and licking her face or hand. I could also picture my bowl for Paulette's food gift and the territory I reigned over within Paulette's territory.

Through a different mind's eye I could visualize the moon shining in the darkness overhead, like the one that night. If I'd hunted, killed, and eaten, and after my pack had taken their allotment, I would have instigated a pack howl. The hunt and the moon were tied to each other. We needed, maybe not needed, but we really appreciated the light of the moon to conduct the nighttime stalking of prey. The urge to howl afterwards was purely emotional. A feeling in the esophagus, a heaviness and, at the same time, a tickle promoted this behavior. I'm sure all wolves have felt it and responded in kind. I yearned to howl for so many reasons. The after dinner howl was one of the reasons I partook of this journey. It was a tremendous physical accompaniment to the central theme: to be as "wolf" as one could possibly be, although I have to admit the theme at that moment was being interrupted by the internal war going on between an overly stimulated brain and an under achieving stomach.

That noisy, empty stomach wasn't getting in the way of my nose, though. I smelled meat, or meat smoke to be more precise. Near the road was a row of buildings. One of them had meat smoke pouring out of the top, near its side and a gathering of many cars with humans getting in and out of them. I had to be very cautious; humans were unpredictable. But I was driven by my hunger to the back of this one building. There, out in the open with its lid standing straight up was a large metal box where the most incredible odor poured into the surrounding air. The smell wasn't at all unlike that of the food Paulette presented to me in my bowl mornings and evenings in my old territory.

Getting to this wondrous bounty would take a bit of skill. One must be invisible and silent. So while crouching low, I crawled through a field of high grass bordering on a black surfaced clearing, hopefully hidden from the humans' view as I made my way toward the large box. Because of my size, I imagined that I'd be able to stand up to it, resting my front paws on its edge, and drag most of its contents near the top out on to the ground for a pleasant but hurried meal.

The obvious problem this posed was, because of my size, humans might react to me in strange and fearful ways. So I waited there, at the edge of the field, until the vehicles and humans stopped coming in such large numbers. The moon that had guided me this hot night had moved from directly over my left ear to directly over the center of my head. In terms of time I had no clue, but my patience was waning as my hunger became unmanageable. Instinct told me to wait til no one was there, but my stomach told me to slink low over to the food box some twenty wolf lengths away.

Slinking should have been natural and effortless. I should have made myself slink as often as possible in life so that the muscles necessary to support my considerable weight could function perfectly in a typical hunting situation. If I'd lived in the wild those muscles would've been there for me. But, as you know, I'm a domesticated wolf, with a name, a collar, and obedience training — hence no strong slinking muscles. So, now, when I really needed to slink, with humans nearby and light sources other than the moon illuminating the entire back of the building, my legs started to shake and I could hold myself up no longer. I quickly ran back to the field and hid. A human yelled in my direction but it stayed near its vehicle. Disappearing into the tall grass I decided to give up on this stationary but dangerous prey.

I felt confused by this hunger. Being used to regular feedings, I wasn't prepared for this painful and disturbing feeling. I made my way parallel to the road with food temptations too dangerous to pursue (none of them living animals, by the way) and focused instead on moving forward, sometimes running when I got scared by humans or vehicles and sometimes trotting at a lazy, leisurely pace, always thinking about food.

As the sun came up, I knew I needed to stop, drink some water, and rest. I had traveled a long way since my nighttime food scare and arrived at a small river in a partially cleared wooded area. I immediately went there to drink. The water was good and pure, and though not a substitute for food, it made me feel a little better. With my head bent to the water, my tail to a path, I heard, over the rushing sound the rapids made, a human running very steadily, to some unknown destination.

I looked up and jerked my head around to watch it, to make sure I wasn't being observed and saw the human run casually away. Then came a small, shiny, chestnut brown dog, walking, sniffing, doing normal dog-like things along this same path. The brown dog was alone and, unlike me, unconcerned.

I slowly moved away from the river, not wanting to be seen even by this little brown dog, and hid in a cluster of bramble bushes a few wolf-lengths from a tree the dog was marking. When he finished, he looked up and sniffed the air. He caught me. He looked around and achieved eye contact, causing a chill to run up and down my spine. Here's me, 155 lbs., six feet from tail's end to snout's beginning, hiding in the brambles experiencing a fright chill, and the little brown dog, say 22 lbs., two and a half feet in length, totally non-committal, taking in the large, silvery animal without any fear or real interest.

What I was hiding from? Was it a fear of this unknown territory? A fear of my own lack of strength? Was it just

canine dementia from lack of food? I hadn't an answer, but that kind of thinking was too dangerous for me to let continue, so I made the decision to come out from behind the bramble bush. At that instant, out of nowhere, a little white dog came ambling along the same path the human and the little brown dog shared. What happened next was new to me. I'd never seen canine behavior of this nature ever before. If canines thought more, or if we were the slightest bit judgmental, we would've considered this behavior perverted.

The little white dog was moving forward, no doubt about that, but oddly, with an altered gait. His legs were stiff, not jointed, and he seemed to glide along the side of the path. His white color was completely off. It wasn't reflecting properly, being dull, as were his eyes. Canines don't have an elaborate repertoire of facial expressions, though our faces do a good job with the few we have, but this little white dog's expression was one I had seen once before when I came across the remains of a dog that had been hit by a vehicle. It lay on the road with a

completely blank expression, teeth showing, and no energy output whatsoever. It was this same blank expression, perhaps mixed with a touch of evil, that little white had. Looking at him face on, I discovered that the main transmitter of his touch of evil look was the length of the lower front teeth sticking up to a ridiculous height, and this with his mouth closed! Needless to say, I experienced another chill. So, back I went behind the bramble bush. I tried to hide a little better this time. I didn't want the little white dog to see me at all.

Little brown dog saw the little white dog and appeared to be getting ready for some social sniffing. Social sniffing, a dog chat of sorts, seemed so strange to me in this case because I immediately sensed something quite the opposite of social from this little white dog, bordering more on the sociopathic side of the spectrum. Yet the little brown dog didn't register the slightest concern. They moved toward each other, and then, (this is the perverted part), little white dog glided up to and under little brown dog's stomach and bit into it. The sound that the little brown dog made let me, and anything within this large territory, know an evil and painful carnage was taking place. Oh, the caninenanity!

Little white was upside down under little brown. Little brown's feeble attempt at fleeing was fruitless because little white simply allowed himself to be dragged along the pathway. There was, oddly, no blood. In short order, little brown fell over and little white, with some difficulty, un-bit his stomach, extricating lower canines that rivaled mine in length. The little brown dog stirred from his position on his side and stood up, stiff legged. His fur no longer shone, his eyes no longer glistened, but his gaze was right on me.

I was so overwhelmed by the viciousness of the attack that I barely realized I was NEXT! When I came to my senses I ran, and fast. Even though exhausted and hungry, I managed to run with incredible speed. Little brown and little white saw me take off, but only little brown gave chase. He'd adopted the stiff legged glide, but he was no match for me.

I ran along the path toward a tower of steel, a train trestle. Ashamedly I ran blindly. I was scared. As I neared the tower and what looked to be an old well opening delineated by stones, I heard a strange murmuring coming from my right. I looked over to a clearing and saw many swaying, growling, murmuring dogs following me with their eyes, but not their heads. None lifted a paw to come after me, maybe because little brown dog was fulfilling that mission, but I sensed that I shouldn't continue forward seeing that the path curved and I didn't know what I'd find. It occurred to me that I was thinking the way my prey would. It's awful being prey, but since I'll never remember this moment, there will be no compassion or mercy if in the future, I ever get to stalk, hunt, kill, and, Dog willing, eat wild prey.

I stopped abruptly, sniffed to the right and smelled danger; and so, being a clever wolf, turned left and ran up a steep hill with a heavily traveled road at the top. Vehicles are, no doubt, a danger too, but I had to go this way. Fear of the swaying masses to my right was quite motivational. The fear gave me some welcome energy and, before I could get my bearings, I found myself past the busy road and in the middle of a quiet neighborhood street. I passed intersection after intersection until I got into a mildly familiar neighborhood and began to forget the bizarre attack and strange dogs in the enchanted forest.

I came to a house with a narrow side path leading down to a small but safe yard. A yard I was truly familiar with. Winnie's yard. My instincts hadn't let me down. A safe haven had been tucked away in the back of my brain and this was it. Not the suburbs, but the city, and after the scene in the park and my journey through the woods and uncharted territory, I felt that I couldn't have landed in a better place.

In the yard, which was entirely fenced in, were many plants and trees, enough to hide behind and get some rest, though I didn't really need to hide anymore. It smelled of cat. Not a problem, believe me, and it also smelled of dog, a living, breathing, shiny dog just beyond the glass back door of this house. I saw, through the full-length window, the eyes of a reddish-tan and white miniature wolf, ears upright and snout of a proper length and proportion.

A miniature wolf? No. It was Winnie, fuming because I was in her space and she was powerless to do anything about it. There was a certain aspect of dog fun in this, but at the same time I wondered if all of this running away was worth it. I wondered if I would ever see Paulette again. I wondered if I had made a gigantic mistake.

My Name Is Nigel and I am a Dogpyre

My dogpyrism began when my primaries, Jim and Jo Anne, accidently left the front door of the house open. We were coming back from a car ride and entered the house, and the open door left just enough room for me to squeeze through and explore Winchester Street on my own.

I trotted down the front steps (which took a while because of an intriguing scent someone had left on the third step), and slowly walked down Winchester Street toward Tatnall. You might say I sauntered, which is the way I usually walk, stopping, sniffing, looking around, just taking it all in. The scent-marks were familiar, and quite frankly, ho-hum. This was proving to be a slightly boring, but nevertheless, pleasant outing.

At Fourteenth Street I turned left simply because the wind was blowing from that direction, bringing with it a decomposing animal odor that was irresistible. It took awhile to get to that odor as I was obligated to inspect each and every marking and the many food morsels along the way. What can I say, a dog's life is made up of morsel

29

moments, territorial marking, and sleep. But the promised decomposing animal was not to be found on Fourteenth Street so I took a quick right turn onto West Street heading toward Brandywine Park.

Crossing Fourteenth Street posed no problem because there were no automobiles. Park Drive, on the other paw, near The Little Church on the Commons was buzzing with fast-moving traffic.

As a confirmed tire chaser, this proved to be the highlight of my outing. When I spotted a tire that seemed particularly animal like, I gauged its speed and started my sprint. I ran into the street alongside the tire and lined myself up so I could bark at it, when all of a sudden the tire froze its circular motion, and out came the loudest scream-screech-roar I'd ever heard. I didn't know tires could make noise. The tire (and the rest of the car) went sideways and came frighteningly close to me. I rightfully panicked and ran onto the sidewalk leading to the stairway down into the park. I'm generally not a fan of stairs, but I navigated this set beautifully and was far away from that awful noise in very short order.

I ran alongside the old millrace, passed the empty dog run, and continued on, slowing slightly because the decomposing animal odor was getting stronger. I slowed down even more when I began to realize that there was more to this odor than just decomposing animals. It had an almost magnetic power.

Moving forward, on my left, was the millrace, filled to the brim with fast-moving water, and on my right, the serenity of the park and further right, the roar of the Brandywine River, rapids and all, which eventually led me to the dirt path that ended at the old well, next to the train trestle. I sensed movement farther down the path, but I wasn't getting the usual odors that normally go with twitchy movements in the trees and shrubs.

Soon I spotted a tremendously large, silver dog with the odor of a superdog. I wondered "could this be a wolf?" But what would a wolf be doing here? He looked a little out of his element, darting in and out of the shrubs with a wild look in his eyes and definitely in need of some self-grooming. He seemed to think he was hiding.

The wolf hadn't spotted me yet, but he soon would, even though the wind was in the wrong direction. I wasn't afraid because there was something else taking up that portion of my mind. Something very much to do with this decomposing animal smell.

I kept along the path toward the train trestle, hyper aware, now, of my sensual intake. I was similarly aware that Jim and Jo Anne weren't here, which seemed odd, but that may have had something to do with squeezing through the front door without them.

As I approached the old well and train trestle, I heard, in the distance, a very low murmur, an eerily disturbing sound that was large and seductive and way beyond my usual set of experiences. Pulled forward by this invisible leash of sound, I trotted along the path to a place where I could see the foot of the train trestle, and then stopped short. What I saw made a Mohawk-like ridge rise from the back of my neck to the tip of my tail. Ahead were fifty to sixty dogs, all shoulder to shoulder, roughly matched by height, slowly swaying from left to right, growling their group growl, and dazedly staring ahead.

I was being summoned, and for some reason, I was not afraid and more than willing to go. The group growl, though intimidating, was at the same time, enticing, and because the dogs were not taking any notice of me I moved into the brush to the foot of a tree, which I marked.

As I completed my marking, Yogi, a white bichon frise and neighborhood friend, glided toward me in the most bizarrely confident manner, not afraid, not friendly, not really anything at all. He saw me and moved closer; close enough for me to notice his dull pallor and strange behavior. There was no energy coming from him. When he was about two Nigel lengths from me I noticed that the other dogs had stopped swaying and growling. They were all lined up in perfect formation, looking directly at me. Their eyes were dull, and their pallor looked exactly like Yogi's.

Yogi continued to glide toward me, no sniffing, no eye contact, no preliminary anything, and rolled over onto his back, wiggled under me and then, OUCH! He sank his teeth into my stomach. I yelped like no dog has ever yelped before, my scream rang throughout the park. I was being drained. Drained of my blood, my sheen, my mind. In five excruciating minutes I was no longer Nigel. I was Dogpyre!

Instantly, as the last drop of blood was sucked into Yogi's fangs, I knew I was no longer part of the living world. I was one of them, the swaying, dull, growling, murmuring mass that occupied the flattened patch of ground at the foot of the train trestle. I had become a being unlike any before, a being with venom for blood.

Everything was different. My vision was hazy. My olfactory sense was completely gone save for the scent of blood I picked up from a nearby squirrel. My teeth, which had never bothered me before, ached. But it was finally my hearing that cemented the belief that I was no longer Nigel. It was now over amplified to an unbearable degree. I heard myself murmur-growl. And at that same moment of sonic realization, my paws were gliding, taking me over to my new mates. I even developed a new feeling for that wolf I

had seen earlier, and glared at him with a hint of evil I had never possessed as Nigel.

None of this was without pain. A sharp torment in my head stimulated each and every murmur and caused me to rock from side to side, as if this noise and swaying would somehow relieve the jabs to my brain.

Trancelike, I stiffened my legs, glided over to my height group, and slipped into the swaying formation next to Bel, a white miniature poodle. Though now shoulder-to-shoulder, we didn't sniff or greet in any way. Accepted or ignored, I didn't know which, I was included in the most noncommittal way.

And that's how I wanted it. These new rules to live by seemed just as normal and reasonable as the old ones. When I added swaying to my murmur-growl, I melted into this mass. No single identity, no id, but part of a great big, dominant dog being, a sixty Dogpyre-strong mass, I but an actor with a new role: to search for blood, to feed and serve some unknown entity, to be Dogpyre.

Paulette Sat Down at Her Desk and Francine Began to Worry

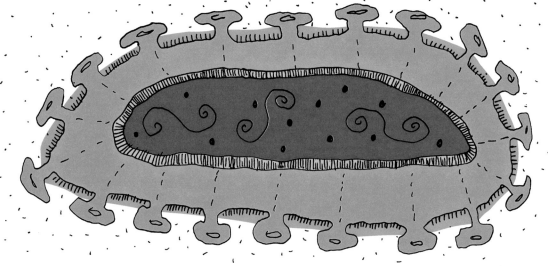

PAULETTE

Paulette sat down at her desk. Her office was in its usual state of chaos, but, as is typical of intelligent people, it was an ordered state of chaos built of hierarchy and status, ranking and chronology, that placed anything to do with Phyto 710 at the top.

She had just gotten off the phone with Allen Samso, a biologist in building P21 where she and Lord Northridge had taken the living and dead bats from Francine's back yard for his expert opinion. The call left her with a feeling of helplessness because, according to Allen, "we haven't seen a structure like this before." She was hoping for a little bit of progress, but there was nothing.

Allen was totally perplexed by the blood samples taken from the bats, and said, "This reminds me of HIV, if you can believe it. Your Phyto 710 has somehow re-structured things. There are anomalies when we do a false-color scan with the electron microscope. I'll email you that micrograph. See what you think. It's a puzzle, Paulette. Did you know about the effect the Phyto has on a macrophage? Anyway, we've been stymied before and always seem to come up with an answer. We'll keep on it," he said, trying to lift her spirits.

She ended the call and put the Blackberry on her desk next to a picture of Parsi, Winnie, Francine and herself taken by Reynaldo in his backyard. A simpler, happier time, to be sure.

FRANCINE

Francine began to worry. She thought she had brought Winnie into the studio with her, but Winnie wasn't there. Then she thought Reynaldo must have taken her.

"Reynaldo, do you have Winnie?" she yelled from her easel as she worked on a french landscape. She usually placed Winnie on the floor to her right, near the palette and taboret. When she turned to mix a color she noticed Winnie wasn't where she was supposed to be.

"No. I was in the basement. I thought you had her," Reynaldo said.

"I've been in my studio. I thought you had her. Is she behind the sofa? She's crawled there before," Francine walked to the top of the stairs and saw that Winnie's wheelchair wasn't in its usual parking spot in the living room.

"Oh no! Reynaldo, she's still in her wheels!" cried Francine.

"The backdoor is open. I'll check the gate," said Reynaldo, running out to the backyard.

"It's open! The gate's open!" he yelled.

They raced out of the gate and down the sidewalk calling her name as they spread out into the neighborhood.

Meanwhile, as Francine and Reynaldo searched for Winnie, Allen Samso picked up his Blackberry. Sweat formed on his brow in his excitement. Nothing like this had come to his lab since he started working there seven years ago.

"Look, Paulette, The HIV theory is completely wrong. This blood is unique. It changes the blood of other mammals. And not over time — instantly! We're still figuring out which groups it will affect, but right now it seems definite that it won't affect humans. What a relief that is for your department. This stuff is odd, though. It'll alter rats and mice, but not our primates. And in canine blood it's magic. We'll have to do some out-of-the-box thinking on this one. I'll be in touch when we have something," Allen ended the call as he ran back to the lab.

Back in the neighborhood Francine and Reynaldo were asking anyone they saw if they had seen Winnie, to no avail.

They swept down 14th Street, left on West Street, then back towards Tatnall, their street. Reynaldo hoped she had decided to return home. As they passed Winchester Street, they noticed a commotion at the far end. Three dogs looked like they were playing together, with a cloud of bats just overhead. One of the dogs, Nigel, pulled out of the pack, and headed straight towards Francine and Reynaldo, the bat cloud followed overhead. The other two dogs appeared to be Parsi and Winnie, and Parsi was about to take a huge bite out of Winnie.

"Parsi, stop!" they screamed, waving their arms as they raced towards Winnie. Nigel and the bats continued forward on a crash course as if Francine and Reynaldo didn't exist.

When Francine and Reynaldo finally reached Winnie and Parsi they couldn't believe their eyes.

When Winnie Met Nigel

Nothing refracts light better than the real thing. Let me re-phrase that. Everything refracts light perfectly, it's just that refractions of "the real thing" seem to be more satisfying. For example, a wax carrot or a real carrot; no contest. Or a stuffed polyester life-size Corgi next to a real one. Again. No contest. So the first thing I noticed about Nigel to clue me in that all was not kosher, was his dullness. Not dullness of spirt (that was always there as far as I'm concerned) but dullness of presence, dullness of eye (matte black, not shiny), and dullness of coat, which was usually a stunning chestnut brown with a nice sheen. Some of us are without sheen, myself included, because of the color and length of our fur. Others, like Nigel, really did shine and it meant something to those who viewed him. It meant health, vigor, and dignity, which led to a tiny bit of respect. But this time something about Nigel was wrong. Something that made my fur stand up, made me want to appear larger than I already was – the word gigantic comes to mind – so that whatever Nigel was thinking, he'd be better off thinking it somewhere else.

I encountered Nigel on a wandering. The gate to the back yard was left askew, so, still in my "wheels," and Reynaldo and Francine now in the kitchen, I strolled down the path by the side of the house, navigated the ramp over the two steps onto the sidewalk, made a left onto Tatnall Street, all in the most unhurried and casual manner, and then another left onto Winchester. I was completely content with this newfound freedom. As a matter of fact I didn't even notice that I was free, mindlessly sniffing, moving forward, stopping, and standing, then moving again. No, let me correct that statement just a little bit. From all outward appearances I was seemingly free, but something inside my head was subtly motivating me to leave my home, and more importantly, my pack. As I pointed out earlier, after the bat bite, I was no longer the same Winnie.

I walked a few yards onto Winchester Street and reached the first tree, which I sniffed. Many dogs had been there in the last few hours and I was just starting to get a sense of who exactly it was when a solitary molecule of Nigel invaded the corner of my nose. While not a full-on dog odor, it was mixed with that awful smell which, for some reason, was always with me. I was so used to referring to this odor as "that awful smell" but, now, in my new state of mind, it wasn't such a bad smell at all.

Nigel was nearly my size physically, but on his best day he was no match for me electrically. I really do exude the alpha rays, I'm known for it, but what's this? He was approaching me at a rapid pace with flaps up exposing all of his upper teeth and most bizarrely, his lower canines were exceedingly long. This is when I noticed the dullness. At two Corgi lengths away I got ready to intimidate him, but was a little confused by this dullness. I had everything in place, as I mentioned earlier, to scare him off. I'd really turned it on, starting with a tremendous show of teeth, and a remarkably impressive growl. I was so wrapped up in how ferocious I was that I didn't notice what Nigel was

actually doing. If I had, I would have been flabbergasted. He rolled onto his back, placed his snout under my belly, under my belly!, and he sank those extra long bottom canines deep inside of me. I, of course, shrieked, and loudly too, and felt a searing pain in my stomach. This was a shriek of arrant terror. Nigel held on with all of his strength while I became weaker and weaker. I couldn't fight back, thanks to my wheelchair, so I tried to move away which only served to drag him along as some sort of mutant growth under my belly.

The pain was as frightening as Nigel's unbound aggression was horrifying. His bite should have resulted in the loss of a lot of blood. I should have been able to see it and smell it. Blood should have been everywhere, but there was none.

Another absence that wasn't going unnoticed was the whereabouts of Reynaldo and Francine. They were nowhere to be seen. Usually they're next to me and would never have

let this happen, but then again, I wandered and didn't realize that that meant I'd be alone. So I had to deal with Nigel myself.

He appeared as neither dog nor cat nor any other animate being, just a something with so many pieces missing from the Nigel puzzle. For example; attacking me? Unheard of. Being dull in appearance? A totally new phenomenon. Attacking while on ones back? Just plain silly (yet it seemed to work). And all of these perceptions and events cloaked in that odd smell. I was alone, scared but detached, completely helpless, and at a loss.

Behind the pain and the confusion of this whole thing and buried deep within, was the awful feeling associated with the fact that Reynaldo and Francine weren't rescuing me, or scaring Nigel away. This was both astonishing and depressing!

Bats! The two-penny variety, like the ones who recently attacked me on the corner of Winchester and

Tatnall, swarmed overhead, and I mean a real swarm of maybe seventy bats blackening the sky directly over Nigel and me. They were about one hundred feet in the air and descending devilishly fast, singing that quick chirp song of which they're so fond.

We were about to be attacked! I began to bark hysterically, still in pain from Nigel's attack and couldn't possibly handle a second attack. Even though I wasn't bleeding, I was getting weaker and weaker by the second, and Nigel kept holding on with those knives in his mouth. The bats were now so close that I could see little differences in their faces. I could see how a momma bat could tell them apart, choose a favorite, be charmed by a certain classical bat profile. But this wasn't the time to get all cuddly about Mr. and Mrs. Bat and their kids. This was the time to panic!

So, why didn't I? What had come over me? Something new had been added to the mix. My mix, that is. I'm not panicking, I'm…accepting! I'm taking it all in and blocking it all out at the same time.

Three bats landed on Nigel. Good. Nigel, not me. Their fangs dug into him with a vengeance. Nigel didn't flinch. Five more landed on him and did the same drill, though a couple of them seemed to be shaving his fur, laying bare his greenish skin. Nigel took notice but didn't let up on me. Then five more landed on him, making thirteen all together, and he un-bit me. I say un-bit because it involved more than just opening

his snout and letting go. He had to extract those two oversized canines slowly so they wouldn't get tangled up in my stomach flesh. Meanwhile, the bats were still focused on Nigel, taking a healthy helping of Nigel nectar, and Nigel was focused on getting out of there. He was being summoned by the higher power who had sent these bat messengers, the higher power soon to be common to us both. I was left lying on the sidewalk in a helpless heap. I couldn't lift my head. My posterior was in the air, elevated by my wheelchair, while my head, front legs, and half my torso were sprawled in a lifeless heap on the sidewalk.

The bats paid no attention to me, possibly because of my altered anatomy or my wheels, but, as I later found out, they were aggressively escorting Nigel down Winchester toward Tatnall Street because he was fresh with new blood and somebody wanted it. The delegation made a right at the corner and continued in the direction of Brandywine Park, disappearing from sight. It was suddenly quiet. Then a bird chirped and I flinched.

Parsifal, who had arrived in our backyard alone and afraid, had become a temporary guest. He trotted up to inspect me. I think I remember him biting Nigel, but I couldn't be sure because I kept blacking out.

My good fortune that he was available to help me was due to Paulette's decision to keep him at our house until she could figure out what to do with his apparent new needs revealed during a special DOGSPEAK retrieval, i.e., "to be a wolf." While not exactly friends, Parsifal had known me since our puppy days. He knew Reynaldo and Francine were my primaries, and his primary, Paulette, had been a part of our lives forever. He also knew that I shouldn't have been out on my own.

Parsi looked me over as if trying to figure something out. His large and ungainly wolf head slowly lowered down to my perfectly sized Corgi head and sniffed. There was no sign of menace. He was simply gathering information. There was just enough doggy-ness left in me to notice that he smelled like a real dog. As a matter of fact, he smelled better than a real dog. He smelled like a wolf. Then the most extraordinary thing happened. He opened his enormous mouth, exposing the most exquisite canines I had ever seen, and clamped them around my neck. I thought, this can't be happening. I didn't really have expectations of normalcy in life, as you might have surmised, but even with my limited set of suppositions, this was just too much! How much could a Corgi take in one afternoon?

Apparently Parsifal was a cut above the obvious. His "bite" wasn't a bite at all. He had me clamped securely but not too tightly. There was a strange feeling of gentleness, a sensitivity you wouldn't expect from such an ungainly animal. The bite had just enough pressure to hold me firmly, but gentle enough to allow some comfort and, most importantly, to let me breath. And on top of it all, with his extra long canines in my neck, I received the most stimulating chills all over my decrepit, wounded body. This was the type of chill one would associate with mating. Of course, mating was off the table at my age, and even more of course, I had been, shall we say "neutralized"(?) in my youth, so I didn't really know where this was coming from. Perhaps it was part of dear Nigel's infusion into my blood that created these odd, and frankly, never familiar, feelings.

But Parsifal had a plan. He saw my predicament and instinctively knew something had to be done. With my neck tightly held, as I have described, he pulled me up from the sidewalk allowing my front legs to support me. Then he started to very gingerly drag me toward home, which was truly awful. For all of his gentleness and sensitivity to my situation, I was in a lot of pain and my front legs were not up to the task. Plus, being dragged by the scruff on ones neck pulled the skin around my throat so tightly that breathing became very difficult. I felt the strong possibility of another fainting spell. But before I could submit to "the vapors," I spotted Francine and Reynaldo running toward us. They must have heard my yelping during the attack.

When they saw Parsifal and I in the classic Giant-Wolf-Having-His-Dinner pose, they became very assertive toward him. It wasn't until they were on top of us that they understood what he was doing. Then they did nothing but shower praise on the maladroit beast, which he rightfully ate up, but which made me physically ill. During this shower of praise, Parsi lost his concentration and dropped me on the sidewalk. I had to lie there and listen to all of this "good Parsi, good Parsi" stuff. Between you and me, I don't know what me sicker, Nigel's attack or the wave of nausea caused by the sight of the halo Parsi was wearing.

Finally they stopped and turned their attention to me. I was a total mess. Holes in my stomach, eyes glazed and dull, tongue hanging out, and barely breathing. Reynaldo lifted me out of the wheelchair, Francine promptly picked it up and we went directly to the station wagon. I rode in Francine's lap as Reynaldo drove us to Dr. Cougar's. Parsi crawled into my usual place in the back, ruining the patina of "Winnie" scent and mucilage I had built up on the windows over the years.

The Great Society

As my former self, Nigel, the gregarious, short, brownish mutt, I would have greeted a good third of the dogs I was about to join. But, instead, my induction into the swaying, murmuring, growling mass of dogitude was painful, un-social, and frankly, pointless. There was absolutely no reason for any Dogpyre to exist. We'd brought no joy to our primaries or to ourselves. Our sole purpose was to suck blood from other animals, especially dogs. We didn't defend one another, or swarm in violent packs on purpose, that would only happen by accident, in some sort of miscommunication from our superior. Dogpyre behavior had reduced us to a group of destructive, movable, objects.

Yes, our purpose was to suck blood from another being, but this was not living, this was merely existing. In our minds, and I speak for all Dogpyres because there could never be a more standardized mind than that of the Dogpyre, two trains of thought were running simultaneously. On one track rode the train of our canine instincts and loyalties; our sense of our primaries; our territories; and of what used to be our food.

The train on the other track, (and this was the dominant train), ran roughshod through our brains and directed us to get in formation, (not information, there'll be no seeking of knowledge here) to sway, murmur-growl, and attack when the need for blood arose. We were not a band of merry dogs running wildly around trees and bushes when we weren't engaged in our profession: blood sucking. We were in lock-step to the drumbeat pounded out by an evil parasite that had taken over our minds and bodies.

Our submissive train, the first one, the good one,

yearned for a return to our real lives. It was repulsed by our new behavior. We were sick at heart all of the time by what we did and yet we couldn't control our evil impulses. We, as canines, had no hope. We weren't scientists like Lord Northridge or Dr. Cougar. We couldn't see the future or even fantasize about it. We couldn't put thoughts together and come up with an idea or a cure. All that was left for Dogpyres was the awful realization that this was our life for eternity.

We swayed, shoulder to shoulder, making our silly sound. We constantly got little blood hunger twinges in our stomachs. Our heads and teeth ached unceasingly. All of our senses were heightened, especially our sense of smell, which had been tweaked to smell blood above all other odors.

At this very moment I was being summoned. My head had been receiving intermittent twinges of sharp pain off and on since I was "turned" by Yogi. Now, though, the twinges were relentless and could only be satisfied by blood. Without any effort or even realization, I was on the move. My legs stiffened and my paws somehow glided over the earth. I had no plan, no strategy, no direction other than forward. As I glided (which I quite liked), I looked straight ahead.

Down the path, next to the millrace, there was absolutely nothing with blood in it. Not a squirrel, bunny, cat, nothing. This didn't really concern me because I had all of eternity to find blood. I had glided out of the park now, past the Little Church on the Commons and into my old neighborhood toward Tatnall Street. I passed Winnie's house and noticed that her backyard gate was open. I didn't pursue that route because some new inner sense, some new extra special Dogpyre equipment, directed me to Winchester Street.

And there Winnie came into view, all by herself, sniffing and walking as best she could in that contraption of hers. She was full of blood. Hot with it. Not only could I not resist her, but there wasn't even the slightest hesitation about what to do next.

She spotted me. Winnie's M.O. was always to intimidate others with some minor snarling and posturing, which she was doing now. But this was wonderful! Her antics were completely meaningless. They didn't even register. Everything that happened next was achieved using a new set of instincts. I was on autodog, and without thinking, my body moved in very close to hers. I've never been this close to Winnie before but I kept moving closer

and flipped my body so that I was under her.

My snout was positioned under her stomach, her softest part, and my aching, lower canines were getting longer. My mouth opened painfully wide, and then CHOMP, my teeth were in Winnie, deep and satisfyingly, and I began to drain her blood.

The sensation was breathtaking! My bad train, my Dogpyre train of thought was so contented that my good train had stopped running. And I wasn't just taking blood selfishly from Winnie, no, no, no, I was generously giving back to her as well. This blood taking was a give and take thing. As her blood rushed into my stomach through my lower canines, something from somewhere in me was being squirted into Winnie at the same time, through those very same teeth. It was a miracle!

But now my good train was running again and I was having some feelings about what was right and what was wrong, and should I stop, and what about Winnie and her health and happiness, as she furiously tried to get away from me.

As I lay on my back, feeding, I looked up past Winnie's stomach to the sky above, and what I saw changed my euphoria to downright hysteria. It was a sky blackened by bats. Possibly hundreds of them diving directly at me. I'd had no experience with bats, but my Dogpyre instinct told me to end the blood taking portion of our program and get back to the "formation".

I tried removing my teeth from Winnie's belly, but it wasn't easy; they were stuck. Concurrently, the bats were sucking my blood. They were also shaving the fur from my precious body. Couldn't they see that I was trying to be a good Nigel Dogpyre, taking my teeth out, stopping the attack? And what's this? What's this? The wolf I saw in the park before I was "turned" was galloping toward me at full speed with his flaps up and his wolfly teeth bared. Before I could shift my position or get my teeth out of Winnie's stomach, he bit me. Bit me hard. I'm a Dogpyre, but I was no match for this.

Sensing my vulnerability from far away, and knowing a good blood drinkin' opportunity when they sensed one, the Bats were taking a lot of my blood, well actually Winnie's, if you want to get technical about it, and they seemed to be injecting something of their own into me. I was severely weakened, and keeping my mouth open was a chore, but, here came another wolf bite. This bite was majestic in every way. I felt a tooth land on the bone in my rear leg. The pain? Let me reflect on the pain. The pain didn't exist. You see, as a Dogpyre, pain isn't a part of our world. Inflict it, yes. Receive it, no. So when the wolf's tooth hit my leg bone I did feel it, but it didn't register as pain or as a warning signal to my brain that something was wrong. My mission was to suck blood and nothing could get in the way of that, unless I was almost full. Then a near logical signal would pass through the Dogpyre synapse-muck in my so-called brain and I'd start making the move to leave. I later realized it was the bats' mission to make this clear and steer me back to my homeland. It was what they did with newbies. Next time I would know on my own when I had overstayed my 'visit.'

So it was quite a large party here on Winchester Street, with a hundred or so bats, Winnie, the wolf, and me, Nigel the Dogpyre. I would have liked to have stayed longer but I really did have to leave. Thanks for everything Mr. Wolf. And to you, the bat brigade, I'd like to give my special thanks because that was quite some welcome into full-fledged Dogpyredom. Winnie? What can I say? As always, it was just wonderful. Thank you, thank you, thank you.

You could see that my brain had been affected by all of this. Even though I couldn't think straight before I initiated my attack on Winnie, now I was a total mess. My Dogpyre instinct (and my flying friends) said to me "you must return to the train trestle and sway, sway, sway." Ok, I was trying, but with the wolf and the bats it was a little difficult.

My teeth were finally out of Winnie and ached intensely. I rolled onto my glidey paws and made haste back to murmur-land, covered with biting bats. My journey couldn't have been more uncomfortable, and I hadn't remembered gliding ever being so hard (even though this was really only my second time). My weakened state had left me in a trance. Sway, sway, sway kept going though my Dogpyre muddled brain and my naked paws (all of my beautiful chestnut brown paw fur had been shaved away by the bats) glided me to my destiny.

It wasn't pleasant, it wasn't satisfying, I haven't moved ahead in my new career to, say, a Dogpyre lieutenant. No, I simply went through hell for no reason whatsoever, inflicted great pain on a neighborhood mate for no reason whatsoever, and ended up a useless, tranced-out lump awaiting my next call to blood. Was this any way to exist? My good train had its doubts.

Night At The Opera

I was caged, but not alone. Dr. Cougar's clinic was filled with caged dogs. I couldn't see them, but I sensed them in the darkened room. Every once in a while, intermittently, a hum issued from a cage here, a cage there, a sort of murmur-growl that was quite catchy.

And I was humming too. Humming a tune of solitude, a tune so mournful that even an ant would cry if it heard it. And I murmured this dirge solely because of a sharp pain between my ears and lower jaw. These sharp pains kept coming and going, and as if that weren't enough, my back legs were moving...both back legs were moving, twitching, strengthening, supporting me as they did in years gone by. I was rejuvenating!

If this were a normal day, if I were normal, I would have been thrilled about my back legs. But this was not a normal day because of the activity going on in my brain. The old Winnie Dumont was packing her bags, recklessly throwing her id, her ego, and her super ego into a ragged and torn shopping bag to be stored in the lower reaches of the right hemisphere of her brain. The new Winnie Dumont had taken over all brain departments, like some kind of demented corporate raider.

So, new Winnie Dumont, what now? How was I to alleviate this pain and desire while being locked up in a cage? How could I express the new inner me? I couldn't just lie there. I had four healthy legs and was compelled to use them. I needed to get out into the world and bite a dog and then...and then what? I hadn't a clue, but I had to get out of here.

My cage was simple enough to open, if you had hands and you were on the other side of it. The latch was actually of the most basic variety. A sliding bolt that I could've maneuvered with my teeth. But what I needed was a co-conspirator, someone who would take pity on this deserving canine specimen. What I needed was a human!

Ask and you shall receive. Or in my case, murmur and someone will come into the kennel and check to see what all the hubbub is about. We were picking up the pace of our

murmuring and it was starting to sound like a barnyard full of cows, enough so that Francine, Dr. Cougar, and Reynaldo all came rushing in to investigate. The room went from dark to light with the flick of a switch.

Too bright. Turn off the lights. All of us Dogpyres were reacting to the light. The many fluorescent lights overhead, pulsating at 120 cycles per second, were killing our little photoreceptors, compounding our headaches and definitely upping our murmur output. We are very sensitive you know.

"What's happening? What's this noise? Winnie, Winnie, sweet Winnie," cried Francine as she crouched down in front of my cage. Dr. Cougar and Reynaldo were on their way over too, but got sidetracked by the condition of my kennel mates. Francine unlatched the bolt and reached in to pet me. She was greeted by my snarling self. Not at all like the old Winnie, but perfectly correct for the new one. Recoiling in what I would describe as a mixture of horror, fear, and the profound hurt of betrayal, her face fell and her eyes teared.

"Kevin, look at this poor guy, his eyes are totally black, and so dull. What is going on?" asked Reynaldo standing with Dr. Cougar in the next aisle.

Dr. Cougar looked into the cage. It was a golden retriever without the usual happy-go-lucky, goofy look on her face. Instead, she wore the look of a predator, growling and baring yellowish teeth in a very aggressive way. Dr. Cougar spoke to her using soothing tones. "It's OK girl. It's OK. Good girl," he whispered. Then he said to Reynaldo, "That seems to be part of this disease. Something completely alters their lymphatic system. The blood samples are showing a decrease in red blood cells and an increase in draculin that eventually invades the brain. I have a hunch that there are lesions on her amygdala." The golden jumped at the door to the cage as Kevin took another look. "I'll need to get serotonin levels on all of these dogs." he said as he lurched back. "I'll bet the test will show those levels are abnormally suppressed. And there's something about this syndrome that's similar to rabies because the parasite invades the host, and just like rabies, it needs a new host to enable it to spread, so it makes the animal unreasonably aggressive."

They moved on to a bulldog named Ran who pushed against his cage door with such ferocity that it was actually bending under the strain. "See, these dogs are compelled to bite another animal. Ran's got to get this parasite into as many hosts as he can," said Kevin. "I hope I can sedate them enough to clean and dress their bat bites. I'm not sure what to use to calm them down."

They walked toward the back of the room looking down onto each caged Dogpyre. All of them were in a similar state; restless, murmuring occasionally, and angry when approached. All had a telltale bat bite or two, usually at mid spine. Kevin and Reynaldo rounded the last cage in the first

43

aisle and came to a teary Francine sitting on the floor, gazing at Winnie.

"It just makes me sick. This is awful. I can't even pet her. She has no idea who I am! And her back legs, she's standing up, she's using them!" she said through her tears. "When we brought her in, when everyone started bringing their sick dogs in, none of them were like this and it's only been a couple of hours. How far will it go?" she asked.

Good question, and how long would I have to be what I wasn't? Some other questions came to mind like; when will they leave? When will they turn out the lights? How can I get out of this cage? And those questions were answered right away. The three of them had decided to go into the clinic's laboratory and leave us to our suffering. In their amazement of my sorry state, they forgot to re-latch my gate, so I quietly trotted out. And just like in a prison movie, I dutifully slid open each and every cage's latch on my way out using my painful, but handy, Dogpyre teeth. Solidarity. It's what we Dogpyres do.

I smoothly walked. Let me say that again. I smoothly walked, using my newly activated back legs, out of our kennel area and nosed around the building (avoiding any place where I could hear voices) until I found a bathroom that conveniently possessed an open window. I simply climbed the toilet, placed my front paws over the windowsill and jumped the eight corgi lengths to the ground, landing on my neck and unnaturally bending my right front leg behind my right ear. I was free. Free but immobile because both my neck and leg were broken. A true disaster for any being excepting, of course, a Dogpyre. Within seconds bones were twitching and mending and I writhed into an upright position, ready to move on to the only place a Dogpyre can feel at home, our spot by the train trestle.

The Well

How did I get down the well? Why did I go there? And what was with this murmuring? I asked these questions in my newly abnormal, Dogpyre way. Not, of course, a clear, concise thought, but simply a rush of uncomfortable chemical synapses speeding down the bumpy and potholed synapse highway. These were very special synapses – Dogpyre synapses – twisted, distorted in that special Dogpyre way, with just a spritz of vitriol, or, more accurately, Phyto 710, to create the perfect Dogpyre synapse that would make me do the things I now did.

Questions demand answers and I have them. Let's start with the well, shall we?

The well. Who knew it even existed. I've been on many a walk with Reynaldo and Francine in this area of Brandywine Park, near the train trestle, and have never seen the opening for it. There's a reason. It was once covered with a wooden lid and then, over the years, a variety of wild growth obscured it. Then, rot had decayed the lid leaving only the brush cover to hide the gaping hole beneath. If you stepped there you'd fall in. But now I was acutely aware of the well's existence, and within the well resided a force that was like a magnet to all Dogpyres. It had absolute power over us and was the reason we existed. And that force had just called, telling me it was my turn to go down the well.

The calling, I say calling for lack of a better word to describe the force I was dealing with, would hit us Dogpyres right between the eyes in the frontal lobe, the part of the brain that tells one to move, as in MOVE NOW! The calling came in the form of pain, excruciating pain, that one quickly learned to alleviate by murmuring while moving toward and eventually going down the well.

Now's a good time for me to explain, briefly, the physiology of a Dogpyre. Briefly, because no one really knows what is going on in this regard, but let's just say that in terms of accepted biological standards, all bets are off. The phyto 710 twist of fate that took place a while back changed the molecular structure of the Dogpyres and the bats that infected them. Basically, we became, in a way, perfect physical specimens. Our bodies could do no wrong. For example, when Nigel was attacked by the squadron of bats the other day, they, correctly, within the normal practice of this type of bat's attack method, shaved off large swaths of his hair, an apparent impediment to a clean bite. It grew back within the hour. And, as you may have remembered, I was no longer paralyzed. All four legs were hale and hardy! That's the Dogpyre guarantee: perfection within the hour or your money back.

I tell you this only to explain the method we used to go down the well. We all did this the same exact way. There are no deviations in the world of the Dogpyre. We were in such lockstep, you'd think we lived in Singapore. First, we'd feel the pain. Then we'd glide on over to the well opening...and jump. Yup, we'd jump.

When I jumped into the well, in my crazy mind, I was doing something as normal as breathing, and I jumped into the well two or three times a day. I traveled about thirty corgi lengths down until I hit the bottom. Fantastic, isn't it? I would hit the bottom on my back, or on all fours, or snout first. No matter how I landed, something broke – legs, jaw, spine – it didn't matter because it was all going to fuse back together, better than new, within the hour. Let me correct that, in this close proximity to *it*, I fused within seconds.

So here was the scene so far. I was lying in a crumpled heap at the bottom of the well, spasmodically twitching as my bones fused and any internal organs repaired themselves. I was in total darkness...except for two dimly glowing orbs trained on me. And this brings us to why I was there.

I was there to give blood.

When one was finished fusing, one didn't just lounge around at the bottom of the well. There was work to do. There were strict procedures and protocols to adhere to. Rules to be obeyed with unbelievable consequences if one didn't comply. I always complied. If I could have thought properly, I would have questioned complying because with instant fusing, who cared what could happen. But, as I said, I always complied. It was simply what a Dogpyre did.

Procedure dictated that one would glide west in the cavernous space that made up the bottom of the well. There was no water. This well had been dry for a century or more. And besides, who needed water when you could have bats? This was bat central. This was the bat cave for all of the infected bats that had spread this beastly affliction. I hadn't the faintest idea how many bats there were, but thousands seemed a reasonable guess. The really interesting feature of the bottom of the well was the possessor of the dimly glowing orbs that had locked onto my dull brown eyes.

First, before I get to the owner, let me tell you about those orbs – the eyes of my liege. Think, for a moment, of the most beautiful shade of blue you could possibly imagine. Now let it glow, just a little bit, so that it would appear to have a candle flame illuminating it from behind. And as you imagine this serene shade of blue, place a piercing, cold, white light possessing the brightness of the sun, condensed into the size of a pinhole, radiating from the center. That is what greeted a Dogpyre when it landed at the bottom of the well. We considered it most attractive.

The owner was my new primary, sad to say, and she was one great big bat, comparable in size to a Corgi. This was MAMA BAT. The queen, the goddess, the boss, and everything else one must obey in this world. I said mama bat because she was constantly giving birth to baby bats. Little Dogpyre bats chirping and playing like any self-respecting infant would, except their play was a little uncomfortable to observe. It consisted of tearing each other apart. So much so that to get to Mama's circle of submission, I was forced to glide over a wing here, a head there, and all manner of things bat. But, being a perfect Dogpyre, I ignored this and presented my humble and obedient self to her. You might have thought I'd quake and shiver in her presence, but you'd be wrong. Does your car quake and shiver when you drive up to the pump at the gas station? It was the same for us. We were devoid of such feelings and fears. We were what we were and we did what we did. A Dogpyre simply took blood and gave blood, and at that moment I was there to give blood.

Fall over please. Thank you. Push your stomach out a little more...that's better. and then "The Bite." It wasn't nice, but it wasn't bad either. I was complying, she was feeding. It was so pointless, the whole process of getting blood just so she could drain us and then produce little Dogpyre bats who

would go out and infect dogs like me to go get more blood for more feedings and just what was the point of that. I hadn't a clue. I didn't even care, I was a dogpye and I was done as a meal for the time being. She'd taken what she needed and had dismissed me. How did I know I was dismissed? She'd removed her teeth from my stomach and closed her eyes. No blue orbs to summon me, so no interest in being near her. As soon as her eyes closed, the power was gone and I was free to leave.

Ever wonder how we got out of our local Bite and Blood? Too simple really. Dogpyre adrenal glands, which were quite large, produced copious amount of adrenaline that gave us the super strength required to climb up the old, rusted, metal rungs embedded in the brickwork on the side of the well shaft.

It was just amazing the way these things fell into place. The queen chose her palace well. Not exactly Buckingham Palace, but a place suitable for a queen of her stature, which was about nineteen inches high. People would be very cramped down here, but for most animals it was just ideal.

My stately queen, this bigger than life fledermaus, so perfectly belonged in such a dark, low-ceilinged, damp, dreary place. Where else to conduct such business? But for me it was closing time and I must leave.

As I crawled upward, using my newly reconditioned back legs, I saw the imperfect circle of light that signaled my journey's end. I was neither relieved to be out of there, nor happy to come "home," since all it meant was that I'd get into my vacant place between Nigel and another short dog, touch shoulders, murmur on those twice daily occasions, and sway. How dumb, and yet, for a Dogpyre, how perfect.

The Willow's Bark is the Dogpyre's Bite

In Brandywine Park near the banks of the Brandywine stands a group of five willow trees. White willows to be exact, not indigenous to Delaware, but happy to be there just the same. They were planted many years ago by one of the park's wealthy benefactors, near the ancient well and train trestle.

The white willow, native to Europe and Asia, is by far the most beautiful of the genus Salix. Year after year the people who use and enjoy Brandywine Park picnic among them, bring guests to admire them, or simply sit near them to contemplate these stately old friends and their surrounding world.

In the bright sunlight of the day the white willows contrast sharply with the intense green of the rest of the foliage. And when the sun has said goodnight, their skin and leaves shimmer silver in the shared summer moonlight that faithfully illuminates their neighbors, the Dogpyres.

While no living thing could be a more unassuming neighbor than a willow tree, the same cannot be said for the Dogpyres. They have discovered the secret of the willow, its bark, and they have stripped each willow from its roots to a height of approximately three feet, laying bare each tree's inner self, open to the dreaded anthracnose fungus.

Why? Why must a Dogpyre be so destructive on top of everything else? Simply because Dogpyres crave relief from the constant pain of the headache by which they are controlled. When you humans have a headache you reach for the aspirin bottle. Analogously, a Dogpyre bites the bark of the willow tree from which aspirin is derived. The salicin therein mixes with the Dogpyre's malefic saliva causing the desired effect, a pain free twenty to thirty minutes.

What the Dogpyre doesn't realize is that with each salicin fix the strength of the Dogpyre syndrome is diminished, so much so that the early bark biters have recovered from their affliction and simply "left the coven" to go home to their masters. Others, who have had only a few bites of bark, have lessened their Dogpyre activities and are responding less to the call of the well.

In the meantime, sad to say, the park's arborist couldn't wrap the trees or protect them in any way because of the ferocity of the gang of dogs still firmly entrenched in Dogpyreism, and still unreasonably aggressive toward anyone or anything that came near their protectorate.

None of this phenomenon had gone unobserved by the fans of the willows or by Lord Northridge who quickly put two and two together. Knowing that "the syndrome," as it had come to be known, was a blood-altering disease, it made perfect sense to him that salicylic acid (aspirin) could have some sort of effect on it. It also explained why some attackees never developed the syndrome and others had only mild symptoms. Unfortunately, Winnie had let all but three of the captured Dogpyres escape from Dr. Cougar's kennel, leaving only conjecture, not scientific evidence, to further the aspirin-as-a-cure theory.

48

Winnie Dumont's Diary

Francine came by today. Tears streamed down her face as she sniffed non-stop into a Kleenex fixed to her nose and cried out, "Winnie, Winnie, Winnie," in a desperate, hopeless voice. I, of course, didn't answer. What a heartless beast I had turned into. Even in my altered state I sensed the futility of their search.

With both of my beloved primaries braving the nastiness of my fellow Dogpyres, and Reynaldo doggedly stepping into the brambles where I was hiding, calling my name in his controlled and calming way, it was all that I could do to stay quietly hidden and not snap at him. And in general, do

the right thing, as in do right by remaining faithful to my ever-weakening Dogpyre credo, and do right by not inflicting my semi-crazed self onto the people I loved so dearly. If they only knew what they were asking for.

During that bizarre week of terror and confusion, they tried to rescue me many times. I would see them at all hours of the day and night. They even came by when I was swaying and snapping, making rescue impossible, causing even more angst for the two of them. Those were repugnant times when my Dogpyre friends and I presented a unified and fearsome front.

Later in the week the discovery of the willow bark permeated the consciousness of my Dogpyre associates. I started my own willow bark regimen, diluting my Dogpyreism with pure dogism, enabling me to understand a little of what Francine and Reynaldo were going through.

As I observed their search, I began to long for home, to get back to our to routine rich with blissful camaraderie, pack-ness, and love. They seemed to be saying to me, no matter what unpalatable state of being I presented, we like you just as you are.

Dogenstein

Have you ever awakened from a nightmare convinced that it was real? I imagine that any animal who dreams, who possesses consciousness, has had this feeling.

Or what if you were living a nightmare? What if you were in a war zone, or you were terminally ill, or constantly abused? The reverse could be true for you. You might have dreamt of sunny, warm days, green rolling hills with grazing cows, food everywhere, and dogs to chase and intimidate. Well, that would have been my dream, but either way, when you woke up it would be a shock. Reality is just plain shocking.

And I was shocked just this past moonless Thursday night in Brandywine Park. It was on that night that I "woke up".

As a Dogpyre, I was subject to all that being a Dogpyre implied. I'd attack dogs for their blood. I'd sway and murmur with my brethren; I'd jump down the well to feed the big bat; I'd regenerate my body no matter what befell it; and, of late, I had developed a passion for willow bark and leaves, just like everyone else here in Dogpyreville.

And like any neighborhood, Dogpyreville had gone through some changes since I had first arrived. Early on, I, like all of my neighbors, was fastidious in my devotion to the Dogpyre credo, attacking, murmuring, growling, snapping, swaying, and in general, being a cog in a massive dog machine designed to feed a ridiculously large bat at the bottom of a well. This was what I lived for. Nary a thought of deviation from this set-in-stone routine did pass my mind.

But as time advanced, around the third day of this conformity, the mind controlling spell began to wane. We no longer held steadfast when someone approached our line-up. We'd scatter and hide and we didn't always heed the call to jump down the well and let the big bat have her way with us. We'd already begun to strip the bark off of the poor willow trees behind us. The more we stripped, the more we became ourselves.

For some this was remarkably good fortune, bringing the end of an era, a return to normalcy, and home. For others it was a disaster. The bark of the willow had a different effect on each of us, leaving many in an in-between state, a very dangerous place to be when you still felt the strong pull of the well-bat requesting your presence.

Rench comes to mind. I know, what a name, Rench, for a dog or anyone, and not even spelled with a 'W." Rench had been a nice companion to someone. He was large and ungainly, and at one time very affable. Our past personas did peek through even while in the deepest throws of Dogpyrism.

Rench possessed a voracious appetite for willow bark, but he was so big, its tonic effect was lost on him. Rench became an in-betweener. And when he got the call to jump down the well, he obeyed, dutifully jumping the fifteen Rench-lengths to the bottom where he landed on his head and broke his neck. And, as a result, no longer a full-on Dogpyre, unable to regenerate his broken bones and concussed brain, died instantly, without pain, without thought, without ever becoming Rench again.

Needless to say, big bat was appropriately angry. She relied on our pumping hearts to help propel our so-called "blood" into her fangs. But as we became more ourselves, we ceased to care. The bat, Dogpyrism, the whole living-away-from-home thing was becoming old. One by one, my mates left the park. One by one there were less of us to heed the call of the well.

For me, waking up from my nightmare created mixed feelings. As I became more Winnie and less "Dogenstein," my paralysis returned and I could no longer regenerate. No in-betweener I, for I had truly and fully become Winnie, the old Winnie who desperately needed her wheels, her Francine and Reynaldo, her backyard, kitchen, bed, food and water dishes, her everything. And speaking of food and water, I was famished and hadn't had a drink for a week.

Without my wheels I could barely move. If I dragged myself down to the river to drink, I'd never get back to where Francine and Reynaldo, or anyone, might find me. My barking ability was gone. Only a hoarse little cough remained. People had stopped walking or running near Dogpyreville a while ago, and the park rangers patrolled the area less often because of our nastiness. Even Francine and Reynaldo stopped trying to find me because I had disappeared so completely. But that was all in the past, and now it was over. Reality had a whole new meaning. I was stuck here. This was my new home.

Yet at that moment, right then, I couldn't worry about my new state of being. If I could, I wouldn't be a dog would I? We didn't worry about the future. We might miss and long for the things of our past, in a very general way, but that would be as far as it went.

My thoughts were now focused on my present state of being which was one of total fatigue. I may as well have lain down and slept. I might even have dreamt a little dream of green rolling hills with grazing cows, food and water everywhere, and maybe even Francine and Reynaldo petting me on my head, between my ears, with a little, but perhaps not too little, perhaps a very big, and deep, massage on my spine, near my back legs that ached so much. And yes, that was exactly what I did.

Tea at Two for Three

"We need to get down there and take a first hand look, maybe hook up a camera and send it down on a cable," said Reynaldo. He was speaking to Kevin and David while sitting at the desk in Kevin's small office at the back of the clinic. In the kennel wing, the three remaining Dogpyres in captivity, the three that Winnie missed in her famous prison escape, were intermittently murmuring.

"Yeah, I agree. We need to know a lot more. I don't think a camera is going to do the trick. It'll be uncontrollable. I've been thinking about using Parsi somehow—get Parsi down the well. He's the only dog we have access to who's proven to be immune to this thing. He's big enough to deal with whatever is down there and he's been great during his retrievals," said David.

"Sounds too dangerous," said Kevin.

"I think it can be done if we're very careful. We'd send Parsi down there as a sort of drone and then get him back to the lab for a retrieval. This way we'll know something about how this thing manipulates the dogs, what it looks like, what else is down there, if anything," said David leaning against a file cabinet upon which rested his glass of iced tea. Tea at two in the afternoon had become a tradition at the clinic since the first days of the syndrome. It was now a week old.

"I'm not so sure I like it. This is really asking a lot of Parsi. And don't forget, we only think Parsi's immune because he's been taking aspirin for his arthritis, we don't know for sure why he didn't get the disease. Anyway, Paulette is never going to go for this," said Kevin, who was propped against his desk. "Also, if you think about it, I don't think Parsi's size will really count for very much since we don't actually know what

to expect down there," he said as he refilled his glass. "And how do we get him down there in the first place? It's pretty deep. If he fell it would be impossible to get him out!"

"No, of course, you're absolutely right, especially about his size and your point about the aspirin. All I can say is it's better than nothing. As for getting him down there, that's not a problem. It's actually done with search and rescue dogs like Belgium Malinois, German Shepherds, and other big dogs in militaries around the world, and quite frequently too," said David as he swirled the ice in his glass. "I'd put him in a k-9 protective suit, harness him and lower him down using the winch on Kevin's jeep. He'll only need to be there for about five minutes then we'll hoist him back up."

"But David, those rescue dogs have been trained for this kind of thing. Parsi will freak out when we try to put him in a suit, let alone lower him down a hole. Plus, don't forget, he's a giant compared to a Shepherd. And just on the legal front, what about the park rangers?" asked Reynaldo.

"Yes, of course. Those are good points. But let's just give it a try. If the suit doesn't fit, or he's nervous about any part of it, we'll think of something new," David said.

"Look you guys, I'm not convinced, but, if we were to do this, and I don't see Paulette going for it, Monday night would be best, when there's no moon. At least we'd be a little stealthy. Parsi should be suited up and ready to drop the minute the jeep's in position. And we'll need to get an idea of what the park rangers' patrol schedule is," said Kevin.

"I have a friend at the state parks and recreation department. I'll try to get her into a conversation about that. She had a paralyzed golden so we talk a lot about Winnie and her wheels. I could casually lead the conversation in the direction of night patrol," said Reynaldo.

"Perfect! And night-time will provide the added benefit of the Dogpyres being less active, at least from what little I have observed. Has anyone noticed? They seem to have lost some of their fierceness since they've been eating the willow bark," asked David.

"Yes, Francine and I have. Our evening searches for Winnie seem to be a little calmer," said Reynaldo.

"Who will talk to Paulette?" asked Kevin.

"Francine and I will do it. That is if Francine feels it's OK. No guarantees on her answer though," said Reynaldo.

David looked up from his smartphone when he heard Reynaldo. "He's going to be quite safe, gentlemen." He motioned for everyone to come over to where he was leaning and showed them what he had googled. They saw a website for Ray Allen, Professional K-9 Equipment.

"I'm going to order the BA1000 Ballistic and Stab Protection K-9 suit, Doggles Eye Protection goggles, and on his head a Tactikka XP Head Lamp by Petzl. Parsi is going to look phenomenal and he's going to be invulnerable, provided everything fits!" He then scrolled down a little to another section in the Ray Allen website. "Kevin, look at this." It was a rappel sling made of 2,000 lb test nylon webbing with an element screwgate metal ring made specifically for winches. As I mentioned, lowering rescue dogs into odd places has been going on for a long time. I think he'll be more then safe down there," he said.

With that the tea party dispersed with each member of the team off to complete their assignments. Kevin to plot a route to the well with the Jeep, Reynaldo, with Francine, to speak to Paulette, and ask his friend about the park ranger night patrols, and Lord David to order about $1,500 worth of commando dog equipment from Ray Allen.

Parsi's Tailor

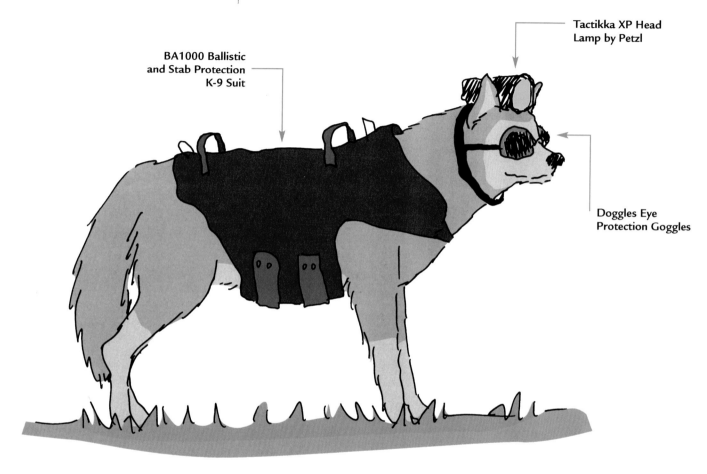

BA1000 Ballistic
and Stab Protection
K-9 Suit

Tactikka XP Head
Lamp by Petzl

Doggles Eye
Protection Goggles

Putting on Parsi's protective suit was nothing less than an ordeal. He was not cooperating and, as was discussed at the time Lord David ordered the equipment, even the largest size was indeed too small. His legs went into the harness without issue, but the straps under his belly were too short and refused to fasten. This would require some tailoring.

"He's a good boy, don't you think?" said Paulette. She was looking back at Parsi who was taking up Winnie's old spot in the rear of Reynaldo's station wagon.

"He's a wonder dog. Both of you are going to be our heroes for a very long time to come," said Francine. She had arranged an emergency visit to her tailor, their destination, by trading a painting for his services.

Francine and Reynaldo's tailor, Isami Nagouchi, was quite traditional, and a true genius with needle and thread. He also had an aversion to dogs. The offer of the painting, one he'd seen at Francine's house a few weeks ago while delivering some garments, stayed in his mind. She'd made an offer he couldn't refuse. Now all he needed to do was to overcome his canine dread.

By the time they had arrived at his shop, a separate section of his elegant home, he had just finished his third sake. Not the heated sake you'd order at your favorite sushi restaurant, this was Junmai Ginjo grade sake, the highest grade available, to be enjoyed slightly chilled. Three ochokos full, the small cups from which sake is traditionally sipped, was all it took to relax Isami enough to deal with the enormous canine about to invade his temple of order. But, then again, to posses Francine's painting was enough to give him the courage necessary to complete the simple alteration on the straps under the protective suit she'd described over the phone. He told himself, just focus on the tailoring, not the wolf.

"Mr. Nagouchi, thank you so much for doing this on such short notice," said Francine as the three of them entered his shop. Isami remained seated, not out of rudeness, but because his sake-weakened legs could no longer be trusted. He smiled broadly, even though, when he thought of having a dog in his house, the old feelings returned, blunted by alcohol, but there just the same.

"You know Reynaldo. And this is Paulette Espin. We left Parsi, Paulette's wolf, out in the car," Said Francine.

"Welcome to you all," Isami said with a slight bow. "It is my pleasure to meet you. Please come in and sit at my table." He managed to rise from his chair without staggering. "May I offer you some sake?" They each took a seat and Isami poured three sakes, wisely not another for himself, and lifted his empty ochoko to toast his guests. "Kanpai," he said, bowing his head slightly. "Now, please tell me why you are putting Parsi in a BA1000?"

"You know about BA1000s?" asked Reynaldo.

"Oh yes. It's an impenetrable dog protection suit. It has been around for many years. I used them in the army. I was a K-9 trainer and handler in Vietnam," he said as they all stared at him in amazement. "My dog, Sumo, was a guard dog. I also trained him for search and rescue, plus cadaver discovery. Sumo was my friend, my close friend. When he died, of old age, I never wanted to have contact with another dog. I didn't want to spoil my memories of him," he said.

"Wait a minute. I can't believe this. You're a dog trainer? We couldn't have come to a better person," said Francine. "I'd love to hear more about your experiences. We all would."

"Well, that part of my life is over now. The K-9 unit was always a pleasureable part of my service, but I had others talents and duties that took up much of my time during the war. I don't like to think of those days, except, of course, my memories of Sumo." He was looking at the floor, a little lost in thought, and then abruptly asked again, "But, why are you putting your wolf into this suit?" Everyone turned to Reynaldo, who took a deep breath and began.

"OK, it's a little strange. Have you heard of the problem in Brandywine Park? The Dogpyres?" asked Reynaldo.

"Yes, I know of it," said Isami.

"Well, our dog Winnie, along with a great many other dogs in the neighborhood, are trapped by this "Dogpyre syndrome," and we think we know its origin. It's at the bottom of a well in the park. The space is too small for a man, so we're sending Parsi down in a rappel sling to take a look," Reynaldo told him.

"I see. But how will you know what he sees?" asked Isami.

"We have a computer program called Dogspeak that will record his observations and translate them into written language. We'll read what he saw and then have a better idea of what's controlling the syndrome," Reynaldo explained.

"I've never heard of such a thing. This is truly phenomenal! I would love to have known what Sumo was thinking. Would it have worked on him?" asked Isami.

"Oh, most certainly. It never fails," replied Reynaldo.

"I'm going to have to let this all sink in," Isami said as he decided on another sake and poured a half portion into his ochoko. He was thinking about Parsi. How powerless a dog was when it came to its own destiny. Then he asked, "Is Parsi trained for this type of work? Has he been in a sling before? He's never worn a suit, correct?"

"No. This will be his first time. Is it important? Can't he just go down there, look around, then come back up?" asked Reynaldo.

Isame rose from the table. He did not have a friendly look on his face and was considering throwing them all out. Then he took a deep breath and centered his thinking on what he considered to be the real problem, how Parsi would feel about the ordeal they were willing to put him through. He sat back down and said quietly, "Look, Ms. Espin, Parsi is your dog, or wolf, and you should not want him to go through this. Why are you letting this happen to him?"

"Oh, Mr. Nagouchi, I have thought about this so much. I really haven't slept a full night since Francine and Reynaldo asked if I would let Parsi do this. But, there's really very little choice. This syndrome is destroying our dogs. They're suffering

terribly, and we've no idea where it's headed. Will it spread to humans? It's already rendered several people temporarily senseless when that fog appeared. Will it happen again? We've got to find out and Parsi is the only available dog we can work with. He's immune to the syndrome, he's big, and can be quite tough. And, really, beyond all of that Mr. Nagouchi, I created the compound at Dupont that caused all of this, so I feel responsible, not that Parsi should suffer for my sins, but should someone else's dog suffer instead? And when I consider the irony that I created this problem and my Parsi didn't become a Dogpyre, but everyone else's dog did, it's the least I can do. It's just the way I see it," Paulette said. She downed her sake and looked at the floor. She was getting sadder by the moment.

Isami took this in and thought for a moment. "I don't understand. You created the compound that started this syndrome?" Isami was thoroughly puzzled by this.

"Yes, I'm a scientist at Dupont and a compound I created was stolen last year and ended up polluting the Brandywine River. A bat, or bats, drank from the river, became infected, and went on to bite and infect the neighborhood dogs," she said with a bit of disgust in her voice.

"I understand now." He gazed at Paulette for a moment as if he were sizing her up, or maybe he was sizing up her explantation. Then he asked, "May I see him? You can let him loose in here, it's OK."

Paulette left to get him. Francine and Reynaldo looked at each other. They were now worried about whether they should continue with their plan.

Reynaldo turned to Isami, "Listen Mr. Nagouchi, it's true. We don't know a thing about any of this equipment, and Paulette only has a small degree of control over Parsi. I think we need your help. Would you help us with him? Or at least help us decide if we're doing the right thing?"

As Reynaldo was speaking, Paulette opened the door and led Parsi into the room. He looked around and sniffed the floor, nervous and panting. Then he walked over to Francine and sniffed her knee. Perhaps a little bit of Winnie was still clinging to the fabric of her jeans. Finally he approached the stranger in the room. A man with a new smell. As Parsi got within a foot of the

stranger, Isami snapped his fingers twice, looked directly into Parsi's eyes, and directed him to sit, using his left hand in what looked like the classic "stay" gesture. This was completely different from what Paulette had learned in dog obedience school.

The wolf sat and stared at Isami, not with malice, but with respect. Then Isami held Parsi's snout below his eyes and whispered something to him.

"What did you say to him?" Asked Paulette.

"Just sounds, noises to make him calm and to trust me. No words, only sounds. This is how we trained them in the war. They would come in from all over the world to be trained, having learned commands in many languages, making language useless, so we developed the sound method," Isami explained. "When are you planning to do this?"

"This Monday night. No moon. We need complete darkness to avoid being caught by the rangers," said Francine.

"I would like to assist. He will need me," said Isami as he rose to take a look at the protective suit Paulette had brought in from the car, Parsi rose too. More sounds were directed toward Parsi, who immediately sat back down. Isami didn't even bother to check on the wolf, he was confident that Parsi would obey his command.

They proceeded to fit the suit on Parsi. Altering the straps would be no problem and everything would be ready by Monday morning. Isami suggested that he deliver the suit and work with Parsi all day, getting him used to the rappelling harness, the suit, the goggles and all of the other foreign items Parsi would be wearing. "He'll need to get used to being hoisted. We don't want him panicking when you need him to be alert. Do you know of anyplace where we can do this?" asked Isami.

"It's not an enclosed place, but there's a place where Kevin can drive his jeep to a lookout over the river. It's directly across from the abandoned Bancroft Mills complex. We could lower and raise Parsi a few times there. Would that work?" asked Reynaldo.

"It doesn't test his tolerance for enclosed spaces," replied Isami "but, at least we'll be able to check the suit straps and rappelling gear. He has to be balanced, so we can get that part done, too."

When they were ready to leave, Isami walked the four of them to the car. Parsi stayed by his side. When it was time to say goodbye, Isami put his hand on Parsi's head and petted him, as he had done innumerable times with Sumo. Overcome with emotion, Isami could no longer speak. He waived goodbye and walked back to the house, feeling a wave of happiness pour over him as he anticipated his next meeting with Parsifal.

Who's Afraid of the Big Bad Wolf?

My quest for freedom brought me to this uncomfortable situation. That bold and daring escape from Paulette and the suburbs only landed me in Winnie's backyard. Fear and inexperience were my downfall, and now just look at me, a silly sight to be sure. I can't imagine why Paulette, whom I know loves me, put me in this ridiculous outfit. For that matter, why would Isami Nagouchi allow such a thing? His commands bedazzled me. His sounds, gestures, and noises were irresistible. I trusted him, even bonded with him, but for some reason, on this day, and especially on this night, he manipulated me into doing things that were not to my liking. And yet, there I was, following his wishes without hesitation.

Attired in the now altered K-9 protection suit and rappelling harness I'd been wearing on and off for most of the day, I was awaiting the addition of the protective eye goggles and the flashlight that would be attached to my head.

Once suiting up was completed we rode to our destination in Dr. Cougar's jeep. I was more than a little anxious.

Dr. Cougar drove, Paulette was in the passenger seat with Mr. Nagouchi in the back. I brought up the rear in the cargo area and part of the back seat, forcing my head next to Isami, who constantly made reassuring noises in my ear, but to no avail. His magic was gone for the time being and I was worried.

Reynaldo, Francine and Lord Northridge rode in the Dumont's station wagon following closely behind. I would have much preferred to have been with them in Winnie's box in the back, maybe even with Winnie.

Our journey that moonless Thursday night, started at Francine and Reynaldo's house in Kevin's fully loaded jeep. It was so fully packed with people and equipment that the roof panels had to be removed so that everything would fit. The night air was warm and humid, but the breeze from our night drive was cooling and would have been seductive on any other night. We travelled down Gilpin Street to the Trolley Square entrance of the park. Just past the tennis courts Kevin killed the lights, drove over the sidewalk and onto a narrow, paved roadway intended for the little Kubota utility vehicles the park rangers used for maintenance. Reynaldo, *et. alia*, followed suit, creating a silently rolling convoy on a secret, at least to me, mission. Then Kevin and Reynaldo turned off their engines and stealthily coasted down the slight decline to the train trestle below. No one made a sound. Even Isami's comfort whispering stopped. What was all of this strange human behavior about?

At the mouth of the well we stopped. The remaining troops, the Dogpyres that hadn't lost that Dogpyre feeling, were only half as threatening as they'd once been. Seeing

their silhouettes lined up near the entrance to the well I instinctively growled from my perch in the Jeep and they scattered. Normally I wouldn't have done this having once been afraid of them, but I was so angry at everything because of my "outfit" and the heat I was retaining, that anything would have maddened me. The only good that came of my growl was a growing confidence, something this wolf was going to need very shortly.

DESCENT

Paulette attached my leash to the rappelling harness. She guided me out of the jeep and over to its front bumper and winch assembly. It was at this point that things became very busy. Everyone gathered around, doing various things such as tightening the straps under my chest, fitting the goggles over my eyes, re-positioning the flashlight on my head that I had managed to relocate around my neck, and attaching the winch cable from the front of the jeep to my harness. It was all too familiar since we'd spent the entire day lowering and raising me over the side of the lookout platform overlooking the river as a sort of dry run for what was about to happen.

I did as they asked, but it was one of the most unusual afternoons I had ever spent, and my awe of humans rose a point or two. There was so much I didn't know about their world and this exercise was an eye opener. After the endless ups and downs of the day, while they were unhooking me from the winch cable, I sensed nervousness in everyone, but couldn't fathom why. We were all together, a pack, and I was thoroughly fond of everyone, trusting them completely. Still, as I mentioned, I was worried, they were nervous, so something must have been up.

Not knowing what was to come next would be my

natural state of affairs. I could only deal with the reality of the moment, just like any canine. So what transpired was similar to the endless ups and downs over the edge of the lookout except, this time, there was no lookout.

Isami led me over to the well's dark, gaping hole of an entrance. I could feel his knuckles on my neck where he was holding my collar. His touch helped me accept what was to come. Then, enclosed in David and Kevin's arms as they lifted me off the ground while aided by the winch, I hovered over the well's opening, feeling the cold, damp air rising from the darkness below. I still didn't know what was about to happen.

David activated the flashlight on my head. The beam shot wildly over the surrounding area, which included an unnerving flash into the eyes of one, lone, hidden Dogpyre, who sat watching the entire ordeal from some distance away.

Then the electric winch started its whirring, a now familiar sound from the day's exercises. I understood. I got it. I was going down the well shaft. This wasn't going to be a pleasant experience. I'm big, the shaft small. I didn't know what was to happen or what I was supposed to be doing.

The descent was very slow, very gentle, but very uncomfortable because the rappelling harness straps dug into my diaphragm making breathing a chore. This was actually a good thing since it was taking my mind off my fear of tight spaces, and this one could not have been tighter.

The descent continued smoothly as I neared the bottom of the well. Looking down, the flashlight followed my eyes and illuminated the space below. The sight was puzzling. A large, white dog, smaller than me, but still large, was lying in an awkward position right where I was to land. I barked, but he wouldn't move. Was he sleeping? Or was he like the deer I've seen lying motionless next to

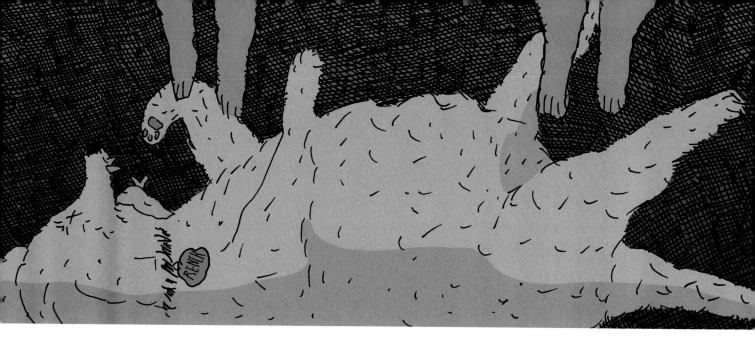

the road in times past? Whatever his circumstance, I was about to land on him. He was quite bloated and exuded an interesting bouquet.

When my entire weight finally came to rest on his taut body, and as the cable slackened and slinked over my side and onto the floor, I moved off of him and onto the debris littering the well's bottom. This rubble consisted of rocks, brick pieces, twigs and leaves, and little bat parts, enough to make an army of bats if they were ever sewn back together. The area I was in was cave-like and pitch black save for the beam of my light.

A strange, potent odor drew me towards a long tunnel opening to the right. I had no interest in looking to my left, which offered no sensory input at all. During this discovery period, my cable, my lifeline continued to slither down, coiling itself at my side like an obedient snake. Though connected, I was free to move in any direction, but my predilection was to get to the source of that odor.

I moved away from my bloated friend and trod over a bat wing here, bat head there, everywhere underfoot a carpet of things baby-bat until I got into a cavern offering a little more room both above and to my sides. Like the well shaft, this area was entirely made up of old, reddish brick. Many broken pieces littered the floor, having fallen over the years from the walls and ceiling, replaced by tree roots and other growths that nature deemed necessary.

ODOR REPORT

My life is ruled by my nose. Sniffing things and assessing their worthiness takes up a large part of my waking day. In the night, when I'm asleep dreaming, I dream of odors. The odors lead to memory-like fantasies that wiggle my eyeballs, twitch my legs, and cause me to whimper. I've never had an odor dream I didn't enjoy on some level. Odor dreams usually have to do with food. Getting it, eating it, or both. But before I reached the

61

bottom, as I was descending deeper into the well, the odor I was sniffing seemed foreign, out of the ordinary, and more than bizarre. I wondered, as I dropped that last leg length, what kind of dream this odor would produce. It certainly wouldn't be a food dream, perhaps carnage of some sort would be on the program.

The large, bloated white dog's odor was all too familiar. The decomposing flesh, some excrement and urine, and the gas associated with such ingredients all mingled to create the scent an inert mammal always produces. I have smelled this odor before, and it passed my odor memory's test for quality and normalcy.

The baby bats' odor was a smell of a different color. There was something sweet, flower-like, yet devastatingly evil about it. This smell had a power, a capability to make one do something quite beyond what one would normally do. This odor had a force to it that made my fur stand on end.

The last odor was the overwhelmingly dominant one. Where the baby bats' odor could be described as an essence, or even a vapor, this last odor was carved of steel. It was the spirit driving all events, all thoughts, all actions down in this black hole. I was having a hard enough time getting my bearings in this dark and dank place, but throw in "the odor" and my brain was simply not mine anymore. My legs took me deeper into the tunnel, closer to the source of this fetor of such strange attractiveness. My thoughts erupted in a myriad of directions, but one, solidly rooted theme kept coming into my mind; attack, kill, eat, and howl. A wolfly instinct was overriding this interference and I began to salivate.

GREETING

As I moved forward, a faint shape gradually emerged from the darkness. It looked from here, with my headlight intermittently illuminating it, like Winnie. It had her approximate size and shape-except for her wheelchair-and a strong likeness to her profile. I was now four of my lengths from this-what was it? A dog? A beast? Without the proper sniffing clues I couldn't tell.

At this point, let me present a canine fact, and I'm not trying to brag here, but my eyes, in terms of light gathering, are better than a human's. I see objects in the dark five times better than you. You see a vast array of colors and I don't, so maybe we're even, but I wouldn't trade my night vision for anything. Having established this one tiny point of superiority (to myself, at least), what I observed in the dimness was definitely a living, breathing animal lying down. At three lengths I could see its eyes. Glowing pinpoints, white hot in appearance, commanding in nature and completely intimidating, aimed straight ahead, not at me.

I didn't stop. I was compelled forward, perhaps a little more forward than I wanted to be, but forward another length and then I stopped. Still feeling wolfy, salivating, thinking thoughts of carnage and victory over my prey, those thoughts were soon overtaken by the demeanor of this beast. It appeared to be at rest, showing no surprise or curiosity at all about my presence. There was no provocation, and obviously no chase, so I couldn't very well attack it. Everything was so confusing. My wolfy feelings about it being my prey quickly dissolved, overridden by my fear of the unknown. This was no ordinary encounter. This was no ordinary animal.

It lifted its head, which had been resting on a few bat carcasses, and turned, giving me a very direct and penetrating look. At that same moment one of its arms, tucked closely to its side, unfolded and revealed itself to be a wing about the same size as me. My one-time prey looked, and smelled, to be

on its way to that inert state I've witnessed so often in the still animals I'd seen by the side of the road. The energy emanating from this creature was losing its power by the second.

Why not try to sniff it, make a connection like I would with any new acquaintance. Let it know I wasn't going to tear it apart. My fear was dying at the same rate as this animal's energy, and there was nothing else to do except stand there and watch whatever was going to happen, happen.

I crouched down and crawled forward, my head level with the beast's head. It never took its eyes off of me. Our eyes were locked. My snout was about a paw's length from its snout when suddenly there was a huge ramping up of energy. The wing from the other side unfolded, and its condition wasn't as grave as the first one. Now that I could see them more clearly, I realized that these wings were actually its arms, webbed to its body, and it was now standing, showing itself to be my equal in every way.

I jumped back. My heart pounded so fiercely that this was the first time I ever knew I had one. Jumping back only yielded a few lengths from this thing and placed my haunches and tail against the wall. With a force I had never encountered, and a pain I had never known existed, it drove its fangs, both upper and lower into my face, just below my right eye and protective goggles. It didn't simply bite and then retreat, it held on like a vise, and sucked out the blood I was supplying in great quantities. Not a drop hit the floor. This creature was a very efficient blood-drinking machine.

After the shock of witnessing the complete transformation of this creature diminished, and after the pain left my face and sank into my psyche, I became angry, and when I'm angry, I don't think, I act. With my new enemy still attached to my face, I shook my head with all of my great strength. I slammed the creature against the wall behind, I smashed it against the ceiling above, and I plowed it into the floor below until it finally let go. I sensed its energy wavering, weakening, then strengthening, but I couldn't worry about its life force any more. There was my anger to satisfy. I was the one on the attack now. I bit into its side and tore off a large piece of flesh near its smallish back legs. It screamed like a siren and I growled like a wolf.

The flesh in my mouth tasted sour and metallic. I could never eat this animal. It was a taste I'd never experienced before, but that didn't matter. This thing had to end. I went for the neck. It saw me coming, and instead of rising up to counter attack, it stood still, waiting for the bite that would end its energy and free it from the torment of a lifetime of evil. Its body quivered in my mouth and then went limp. Its eyes faded from piercing white to black. One easy, unencumbered bite to the neck, one entire body-lift and shake, and it was over. The energy was off. The eyes were dark. The creature was still.

I was still too, flooded with strong emotional feelings about what had just happened. I thought about this animal existing in its "special" way without asking to exist, and now here it was uselessly inert, wasted as a carcass since I wasn't going to eat it. It gave me a feeling similar to worrying, a something-isn't-quite-right feeling, and I howled. I howled with a mournful sadness, not the prideful howl that I had been yearning to do all my life, but rather a howl full of wolf tears.

My cable began to tighten. I was being pulled back to the opening. I trotted along the dark tunnel, illuminated by my trusty headlight. When I reached the large white dog I barked, climbed up on him and waited for the cable to tense up and lift me back to my people, my food, my world.

My Best Thursday Night Ever

I could hear tires crunching on the gravel pathway from quite a distance. It was a welcome new sound breaking the tedium of chirping birds and rustling squirrels. No more murmurs, no more growls to keep me company, I was alone with the perfectly natural sounds of the woods and the river.

Oh, the river! All of that water, so far away. The utter torment of thirst, more than hunger, was driving me mad. Yet I couldn't make that crawl no matter how much I wanted to. It didn't matter that no one would ever find me here, down by the water's edge. I wanted that water, but I didn't have the strength to pull myself there.

The gravel crunching stopped. Two vehicles appeared, single file, and stealthily rolled over to Big Bat's well. My hopes lifted a bit. Voices murmured through the darkness, car doors quietly opened and just as quietly clicked shut. Familiar scents wafted toward me and images of Dr. Cougar, Paulette, Lord Northridge, and Parsi formed in my mind. Then a miracle occurred. I smelled Francine and Reynaldo. I smelled their clothes, their bodies, our house, my world. It all hit me so quickly and I wanted to bark to them, to say "I'm over here!" but I was too weak for my signature, loud bark. I tried my cough-bark, but they couldn't hear that either. I couldn't even hear me. Then I tried a whimper, but that was even more useless, and humiliating. All I could do was lie there and hope.

They clustered around Parsi. He looked odd. His coat was completely dark and smooth, and strange things were being placed on his head. I could tell he didn't like this, though he was cooperating. He was deferring to a strange man, doing his bidding as the others watched. The man put a light on top of poor Parsi's head and for a brief second it shown on me. I raised my head and coughed, but my moment in the spotlight was over in a flash.

The next thing that happened was very un-Parsi like. Lord Northridge and Dr. Cougar lifted him up as if they were planning to carry him somewhere. But instead, he was slowly lowered into the dreaded well, without the miracle of Dogpyrism to heal him when he hit bottom. Poor Parsi. I'll never see him again.

The rest of the group moved to the well opening, looking down, shining flashlights, and keeping silent. Their backs were to me. They were focused on Parsi.

I had to get Francine's attention. My last reserve of energy was quickly draining from my body. The pain in my legs and my overbearing thirst were eating me up fast. Since my barking was too weak, and whimpering was equivalent to silence, I thought of Parsi and how, on occasion, he would howl late at night. When he howled, I usually joined in, quite involuntarily. It would pour out of me from a different place than my bark. I knew there was nothing left to do except make this howl work or perish.

I inhaled a large breath of fresh night air, lifted my head like Parsi would, thought a thought of ancient dogdom and let go with the most mournful howl I could create. It was beautiful, a perfect howl, richly endowed with my feelings of loneliness, pain, sadness, and a large helping of general, everyday emotions all wrapped up in this loud, lingering sound, a sound that shrouded the woods, that silenced the birds and the squirrels, a sound that made my primaries stop looking down at Parsi and turn around to look directly at me...WINNIE.

"WINNIE!!!" Francine shrieked. "Winnie, Winnie, Winnie." She cried as she ran over and picked me up in her arms. Tears streaked her face and yet, she was smiling too. It was a new look and I liked it. She kept hugging me and squeezing my body. I also received several kisses. I was in heaven! Only one thing could have made me happier. Water. If we could just go over to the river everything would be perfect.

Instead we went over to the well. Everyone greeted me with the most enthusiastic greetings I have ever received. Even the strange man gave me a bit of attention, though what kind of attention I couldn't quite figure out. He made some sort of noise and a funny hand gesture that was lost on me.

Anyway, no one had water or treats so I was simultaneously happy and miserable in Francine's arms. Then Reynaldo ran to the station wagon and came back with a bottle of water, my travel water dish and a bunch of treats. I almost passed out with joy. He held the water up to my snout while I was still in Francine's arms and I drank. Not as much as I wanted to, but enough to remember what water was all about. Next, a few treats, one right after the other. This truly was heaven. This was paradise. This was my best Thursday night ever!

My Worst Friday Ever

After an entire week of jumping down the well, breaking bones and organs, then re-inventing myself, it was nice to just lie down under the dining room table, fall in and out of sleep, and listen to everyone babble on about the events of the evening.

My own, personal, guest this Thursday night was Parsi...whose given name is Parsifal, derived from the Arabic Fal Parsi meaning "pure fool." He is nothing of the sort however. Parsi was the focus of the conversation and his ears twitched constantly with each mention of his name.

Lying next to me, my right hip touching his left leg, I sensed his exhaustion as I watched his head bob to the carpet with slowly closing eyes, then lift up in a startled rush. Often the hand of the stranger, now known to me as Isami, would reach for Parsi's head and give it a pat, or gentle ear grab. I was fine with this since I was too far away to be petted by him, and, besides, I already had enough friends.

The conversation was cheerful, but stilted by exhaustion. They spoke of pulling Parsi up from the bottom of the well when they heard his howl, marveling at how clever he was, but I know it was an idea he must have gotten from my howl moments before. They commented on his facial wound that bled and bled until Kevin could clean, suture, and bandage it. And they spoke of the Dogpyre syndrome, of how it died down and finally ended with the demise of the big bat.

Francine put her foot on my neck, lightly rubbing me. She wanted to know more about Paulette's research at the lab. Paulette wanted to tell her too, but, "Ah, Francine, listen, I want to tell all of you everything, but I can't, it's become top secret. I'll tell you one thing. The government's involved in our research. The lab is filled with CIA types. They're everywhere. It's a little intimidating. I'm not allowed to discuss anything having to do with the Dogpyre syndrome outside the lab."

"When did all this happen?" asked Lord Northridge.

"Just this morning. I'm sorry I couldn't say anything, but they were quite clear," she replied. "But I feel you have a right to know a little bit after what we've done tonight."

"Well, I think Kevin and I shall soldier on with the research we've begun. Right Kevin?" asked Lord Northridge.

"You couldn't be more right. What's the big mystery? Why is the CIA even remotely concerned with this?" asked Kevin.

"Here's all I'm going to say about it, and you didn't hear it from me, but, and please don't do a retrieval on Winnie and Parsi either because I know they're listening, but here's the thing. You know how the Dogpyres were able to repair themselves? To regenerate? Well, the government thinks that might come in handy some day. OK! That's it! That's all I'm going to say. Use your imaginations. I have definitely said enough." They glanced at one-another as Paulette stifled a yawn and rose from

her chair. Everyone else was tired too and took Paulette's cue to leave. Reynaldo said something funny and everyone laughed, making the sounds of people being happy and contented. Sounds I was so happy to hear again.

And that was pretty much how my best-Thursday-night-ever ended. I remained under the table as Parsi got up and left with Paulette and everyone else, who hugged and said their goodbyes. I knew I was in for a quiet and restful night. I knew that Reynaldo and Francine, who were so happy to have me back, would be very attentive.

I also had a feeling — or was it an instinct — about tomorrow, Friday. It was a bad feeling. It wasn't a vestige of Dogpyrism coming back to haunt me, but something from my normal routine Corgi life. Something I had heard casually mentioned during our ride back from Dogpyreville earlier this evening. It was just one word, spoken quickly within a group of words, one word amongst the ten or so that I recognize whenever they're spoken. One word, the sound of which made me physically ill...

From page 6:

* DOGSPEAK 1.7

On occasion, or maybe all the time, I simply can't remember, I tell you that I'm a moment-to-moment being. No short or long term memory, just reactions to stimuli based largely on hard-wired instinct that mimics memory, like staying away from something burning hot, even when it isn't, might be an example, or of always being weary of lemons, might be another.

As you may remember, if you've read about my previous adventure, I've communicated to you through the use of the animal to human translation program called DOGSPEAK. That past group of translations, referred to in the lab as retrievals, was the result of DOGSPEAK v. 1.0, the very first iteration of the program.

The version used for this group of retrievals is 1.7. When DOGSPEAK went from 1.0 to 1.7 it, of course, meant nothing to me. I still have to wear the stereotactic cap and I still have to lie very still. But the new and improved DOGSPEAK designated 1.7 meant a lot to Lord David Northridge and Reynaldo Dumont, the originators of DOGSPEAK. To them it meant that my remembrance of words, sentences, whole conversations, could now be retrieved and translated into what you have just read. Let me point out here and now, that reading is the key word in this discussion. DOGSPEAK doesn't turn me into a "talking dog", and don't even think of asking me a question. I can't understand you, so you'll not get an answer. Oh sure, you can ask me if I want to go outside, want to eat, etc. or any of the other stock phrases that are understandable because of vocal inflection, your body language, and, of course, the context in which these phrases were asked. But don't ask me "what did you do next?" or "how did you feel when we didn't take you in the car yesterday?" or anything of that nature, I'll just look at you hoping you were talking about food.

I, and all dogs, have the equivalent of a photographic memory (we can't use it for anything, but it's there, waiting for evolution to unlock its magic). That fact, combined with DOGSPEAK's great facility for handling smell, sight, hearing, and touch has enhanced its ability to make something out of all it takes in (similar to what I naturally do, when you think about it).

DOGSPEAK 1.7, capitalizing on this, and using the profile that's in my "Winnie" file along with the online thesauruses, dictionaries, and encyclopedias, now does a much better job of creating the story, so-to-speak, than the old version. And a new algorithm, based on the design principles of microformats used in HTML5, has been added to act as a logic accelerator. It takes facts from its own memory bank and "conjectures" the outcome. For example, pretend I have the thought: two carrots plus two carrots (not an uncommon thought for me). It will not only come up with the sum of four carrots, it will also report my sense of privilege and entitlement because I have just manipulated my primary (the most likely source of carrots) into a food-related action benefiting me.

You may or may not notice the difference between the old version and this new one because Reynaldo did such a wonderful job of decifering what those retrievals were trying to reveal. Now version 1.7 actually does the whole job and, from what I have overheard, is much more accurate, utilizing only my, or any animal's, excepting parrots, input without relying on human intervention, and all of this without any hint of anthropomorphization (a word I would never use, by the way).

Oh, and I can't remember, did I tell you I'm a moment-to-moment being?